SWEET VALLEY TWINS AND FRIENDS

Jessica the Nerd

Written by
Jamie Suzanne

Created by
FRANCINE PASCAL

A BANTAM SKYLARK BOOK
NEW YORK · TORONTO · LONDON · SYDNEY · AUCKLAND

RL 4, 008–012

JESSICA THE NERD
A Bantam Skylark Book / August 1992

Sweet Valley High® and Sweet Valley Twins and Friends are
trademarks of Francine Pascal

Conceived by Francine Pascal

Produced by Daniel Weiss Associates, Inc.
33 West 17th Street
New York, NY 10011

Cover art by James Mathewuse

Skylark Books is a registered trademark of Bantam Books, a division of
Bantam Doubleday Dell Publishing Group, Inc.
Registered in U.S. Patent and Trademark Office and elsewhere.

ISBN 0-553-15963-1

Published simultaneously in the United States and Canada

Bantam Books are published by Bantam Books, a division of Bantam
Doubleday Dell Publishing Group, Inc. Its trademark, consisting of
the words "Bantam Books" and the portrayal of a rooster, is Registered
in U.S. Patent and Trademark Office and in other countries. Marca
Registrada. Bantam Books, 666 Fifth Avenue, New York, New York
10103.

PRINTED IN THE UNITED STATES OF AMERICA

CWO   0 9 8 7 6 5 4 3 2 1

Jessica
the
Nerd

Unicorn or dweeb?

"Listen to me, Jessica Wakefield," Janet said angrily. "It's impossible to be both a Unicorn and a dweeb. You're going to have to choose between SOAR! and us."

"Janet, this isn't fair!" Jessica exclaimed.

"I'm giving you two days to decide," Janet said. "We'll have an emergency meeting on Saturday, and you can announce your decision then. It's up to you. Do you want to be a Unicorn—or a social outcast?"

Jessica jumped up and grabbed her backpack. "I can't believe you're doing this to me, Janet," she cried. "I've always been a loyal Unicorn!"

"Well, now you're a loyal dweeb, too," Ellen said.

"This is ridiculous!" Jessica protested.

"It's SOAR! or the Unicorns," Janet said firmly. "You can't have both. You decide."

Bantam Skylark Books in the SWEET VALLEY TWINS AND FRIENDS series. Ask your bookseller for the books you have missed.

One

"Here's another detention slip to add to your collection, Jessica. Congratulations."

Jessica Wakefield reached for the familiar yellow piece of paper and sighed. "I was only a few seconds late, Mrs. Arnette," she argued.

Mrs. Arnette glanced at the clock on the wall. "One hundred and twenty seconds, to be exact."

"I hate Mondays," Jessica muttered as she took her seat next to her twin sister, Elizabeth.

"Too bad, Jess," Elizabeth whispered sympathetically. "How many detentions does that make this month?"

"I think I just set a new record for Sweet Valley Middle School."

"Now, as I was saying before we were so rudely interrupted," Mrs. Arnette said, casting an annoyed look at Jessica, "we won't be having our regular social studies lesson today."

A few people applauded, but they stopped quickly at the sight of Mrs. Arnette's frown. "Instead," the teacher continued, "you'll be taking an aptitude test for the SOAR! program you learned about in the special assembly last Friday."

The whole class seemed to groan at once. "That's *worse* than social studies," Jessica whispered.

Mrs. Arnette held up a warning finger, and the class quieted down again. "As I'm sure you all remember, SOAR!, which stands for Science Offers Awesome Rewards, is a special two-week program of intensive science study. Those of you who do well on this test will be selected to participate in the program."

Jessica wrinkled her nose. "She means it's a nerd detector test," she whispered to Elizabeth.

"Would you like to share your insight about the program with the rest of us, Jessica?" Mrs. Arnette inquired.

"I was just wondering if we'll be graded on the test," Jessica said politely. It wasn't exactly the truth, but the question *had* crossed her mind.

Mrs. Arnette shook her head. "No grades. Just relax and have a good time."

Yeah, right, Jessica thought to herself. Have

fun taking a science test? The day that happened, she'd sign up for the Future Nerds of America Club.

"By the way," Mrs. Arnette added, "you sixth graders aren't the only ones taking the SOAR! test this period. All the students at Sweet Valley Middle School will be taking it. The names of those selected for the program will be announced on Thursday." She walked over to a storage cabinet and pulled out a stack of tests. "The questions are in these booklets," she said. "Please use a number-two pencil to fill in the appropriate circle for each question on the answer sheet."

As Mrs. Arnette started to pass out the tests, Jessica let out a long sigh. "What a way to start the week," she moaned.

"Come on, Jess," Elizabeth said. "The test might not be so bad." She reached into her book bag for a pencil. "I hope I do well on it," she added. "The SOAR! program sounds like a lot of fun."

Jessica laughed. "If that's your idea of fun, Lizzie, we really need to see about getting you a life."

At moments like this, it was hard for Jessica to believe that she and Elizabeth were even sisters, let alone identical twins. When they wanted to, the twins could look so much alike that even people who knew them well had a tough time telling them apart. They both had shiny blond hair and sparkling blue-green eyes, and each twin had a dimple in her left cheek.

But sometimes it seemed as if their looks were all they had in common. Jessica's favorite activity was hanging out with the other members of the Unicorn Club, a group of the prettiest and most popular girls at school. Just so nobody forgot how important they were, the Unicorns always tried to wear at least one item of purple clothing every day, since purple was the color of royalty. Unicorn meetings always featured discussions of boys, makeup tips, fashion trends, and movie stars.

Elizabeth wasn't a member of the Unicorns. In fact, she'd nicknamed them "the Snob Squad." She enjoyed reading and doing her schoolwork and spent a lot of her free time working on the *Sweet Valley Sixers*, the sixth-grade newspaper she had helped start. Jessica loved her twin dearly, but she had to admit her sister could be a little dull sometimes. Only Elizabeth could be excited about something that sounded as boring as SOAR!

Jessica wrote her name on the front of her test booklet. "I suppose this beats listening to one of Mrs. Arnette's lullaby lectures," she whispered to Elizabeth. "You know—the ones that put you to sleep in the first five minutes."

Elizabeth laughed. "True. And look on the bright side. We're not being graded."

"You may begin your tests, class," Mrs. Arnette announced.

Jessica opened her booklet and glanced at the first page. There was a drawing of something called an "ecosystem." The picture showed a forest, plants, animals, and a lake. Below the picture were several questions about how different parts of the ecosystem depended on each other to survive.

Jessica stared at the drawing. It was like a little puzzle, in which all the parts had to fit together just right. She reached for her answer sheet.

It was a miracle. She was certain she actually knew the answer to the first question.

"I don't see why we need to take a test to find out who the science nerds are," Lila Fowler complained as she sat down at the Unicorner, the table where all the Unicorns gathered for lunch. Lila, whose father was one of the wealthiest people in Sweet Valley, was Jessica's closest friend after Elizabeth.

"Me neither," said Ellen Riteman, another sixth-grade Unicorn. "It's simple. Just look for the guys with pocket protectors."

"And highwater pants," Jessica added as she opened a bag of potato chips.

"Like Lloyd Benson," suggested Tamara Chase, an eighth-grade Unicorn. "He practically lives in that T-shirt that says *Physics Is Your Friend*."

"Lloyd's a real fashion trend-setter," Lila said, rolling her eyes.

"All I can say is, thank goodness we weren't graded on those things!" Mandy Miller shook her head. "I thought those questions were really hard."

"They weren't so bad," Jessica said. "Not compared to most tests. They were a lot easier than the English test I took last week."

"You thought they were *easy*?" Lila exclaimed. She cast a doubtful look at Jessica. "Come to think of it, you *did* finish awfully quickly. I just figured you were taking wild guesses."

"That's what I did," Ellen admitted. "I'd answer A's for a while, then B's, then C's. I ended up with a really nice dot picture."

Jessica grinned. "I'll take a test you don't have to study for *any* day." She glanced over at Janet Howell, an eighth grader who was president of the Unicorns. "What'd you think of it, Janet?"

"What?" Janet asked dreamily as she munched on a carrot stick.

"The geek test. What did you think of it?"

"Oh," Janet murmured. "I thought it was gorgeous."

Jessica stifled a laugh. "Gorgeous, huh?"

"Awesome," Janet said, staring off into space.

Mary Wallace nudged Janet in the ribs. "Earth to Janet."

"What's she staring at, anyway?" Lila asked, craning her neck.

"Not what," Belinda Layton corrected. "She's looking at a *who*."

"Which who?" Ellen demanded.

"Denny Jacobson," Mary replied. "A major hunk."

At the mention of Denny's name, Janet came to life. "Denny," she cooed. "Isn't that the most perfect name you ever heard?"

"Uh-oh," Jessica said. "She's got it bad."

Mary smiled. "He's in Janet's science class." She shrugged. "I have to admit, he *is* adorable."

Jessica glanced over at the table where Denny was sitting with a bunch of his friends from the football team. He was tall, with thick wavy brown hair and dark brown eyes. Jessica couldn't help agreeing that Denny Jacobson was gorgeous, but she hoped that Janet would come out of her coma soon. They had important Unicorn business to discuss.

"Janet, don't you think we should talk about the Boosters routine for the district basketball game?" Jessica asked. The Boosters was the school's cheering and baton squad. Except for

Winston Egbert and Amy Sutton, all of the members of the Boosters squad were Unicorns.

Janet finally managed to tear her gaze away from Denny. "Did you say something, Jess?"

"I was asking about the new Boosters routine," Jessica prompted her.

"Oh," Janet said. "Well, I talked to Amy on Friday, and she agreed to put together a solo baton number. She said she was going to start working on it over the weekend."

"Why Amy?" Ellen asked, pouting.

"Because she's the best twirler on the squad," Mandy said. "Even if she *isn't* a Unicorn."

"Mandy's right, Ellen," Lila agreed. "I mean, I'm sure any of us could be as good as Amy. We've just got more of a social life than she does, so we don't have as much time to practice."

"So are we going to have to schedule extra Boosters practices, Janet?" Jessica asked.

Janet didn't answer. She was staring at Denny again.

Jessica rolled her eyes. "Janet," she said. "Can I have your chocolate cake?"

"Wonderful," Janet murmured, her eyes still glued on Denny. "Just wonderful."

Jessica grinned at Lila. "True love," she said, reaching for Janet's cake. "Isn't it great?"

Two

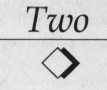

"Exciting news, people!" Mr. Davis announced Thursday morning during homeroom. "I've just received the official results of the SOAR! aptitude test."

"You know what SOAR! really stands for, don't you?" Jessica whispered to Lila, who was sitting in front of her. "Seriously Obnoxious And Repulsive."

Lila giggled.

Mr. Davis scanned the list and smiled. "I'm very pleased to see so many of you on this list. It's a wonderful honor to be selected for this program. As I call out your names, I'd like each of you to stand up so we can give you a big round of applause."

"How humiliating," Jessica said under her

breath. "Why not just make them all wear big signs that say *'I'm a Loser'*?"

"I think we need a drum roll here," Mr. Davis said.

Jessica shook her head. Mr. Davis could get pretty corny sometimes. Several of the boys seemed to think a drum roll was a great idea, however. They began pounding their fists on the tops of their desks.

"And the winners are—" Mr. Davis paused dramatically. "Cammi Adams," he called. "Cammi, come on, stand up so everyone can give you a big hand."

The class applauded as Cammi stood and smiled shyly.

"Big surprise," Jessica whispered. Cammi was a classic nerd, after all.

"Lloyd Benson," Mr. Davis continued. "Peter DeHaven, Winston Egbert—"

When Winston heard his name, he jumped up onto his chair and took a low bow. "I am deeply honored," he said with a grin. "And—"

"Thank you, Mr. Egbert," Mr. Davis interrupted. "I think we get the idea."

Jessica couldn't help laughing. Ever since Winston had joined the Boosters, he'd really come out of his shell. He was turning into a regular ham.

"Randy Mason, Ken Matthews, Melissa McCormick, Tom McKay, Julie Porter—"

"Now he's getting into the Model Student crowd," Lila whispered to Jessica.

Jessica nodded. Elizabeth's name was sure to pop up soon.

"Maria Slater, Elizabeth Wakefield—"

Jessica glanced over at Elizabeth, who was beaming.

Mr. Davis took a deep breath. "And last, but certainly not least, Jessica Wakefield and Todd Wilkins."

"Elizabeth will be glad that Todd made it," Jessica whispered to Lila.

Then she noticed that for some strange reason, Lila was staring at her. As a matter of fact, Lila's mouth was open so wide that Jessica could practically see her tonsils. "Why are you looking at me like that?" she demanded.

"Jessica, stand up and take your bow," Mr. Davis urged.

Jessica looked up in surprise. "Why would I want to do that?"

"Because he just called your name, Jess!" Lila hissed.

"Come on, Jessica, don't be shy," Mr. Davis said.

"*I'm* on that list? *I'm* in SOAR!?" Jessica exclaimed in dismay. "There must be some mistake!"

"Nope." Mr. Davis held up his list. "It's right here in black and white."

"Let me see that thing," Jessica said.

As soon as she stood up, the class burst into applause. "Stop it!" she shouted, spinning around.

"No need to be modest, Jessica," Mr. Davis assured her. "You might as well enjoy your moment of glory."

"Glory?" Jessica echoed. "Moment of humiliation is more like it." She stomped up to Mr. Davis's desk and peered over his shoulder at the list of SOAR! participants. To her horror, there was her name, right beneath Elizabeth's.

"This has got to be a mistake," Jessica moaned. "I *hate* science. Only geeks like—" She stopped herself in midsentence when she saw Mr. Davis's frown.

"Why don't you take your seat now, Jessica," he suggested. "I've got some other announcements to read."

"But this is *horrible*!" Jessica said. "I can't spend two whole weeks in science class."

Mr. Davis shook his head. "My heart goes out to you, Jessica," he said, but she had a feeling he didn't really mean it.

Jessica walked slowly back down the aisle and

slumped into her seat. *This isn't really happening,* she told herself.

"Congrats, Jess," Lila said, twisting around. She had a very annoying grin on her face. "You must be so proud."

When homeroom was over, Jessica stomped out of the room. Lila and Ellen caught up with her in the hallway. "I am not going to take that nerd class," Jessica vowed angrily. "Never in a million years."

"Hey, congratulations, Jessica," Winston said as he walked over with Randy and Lloyd. He gave her a hearty pat on the back. "So I guess you're one of us now, huh?"

"Us?"

"You know." Winston grinned. "Us geeks!"

The three boys walked away, laughing loudly.

"See?" Jessica wailed to her friends. "See what I mean? This is the most embarrassing moment of my entire life!"

"Jessica!" Elizabeth called, rushing over with Melissa and Maria. "Can you believe we're both in SOAR!?"

"No," Jessica said flatly, making a face. "I can't."

"Come on, Jessica," Maria urged. "Give it a chance. You never know, you might actually have fun."

"I know it came as kind of a shock, Jess," Elizabeth said, smiling. "But you should be proud."

"I don't blame Jessica," said Brooke Dennis, who had just joined the group. "I hate science, too."

Jessica nodded. "That's why I'm sure this is all a mistake," she said. "How could someone who hates science end up in SOAR!? It doesn't make sense."

"It seems kind of unlikely that they made a mistake, doesn't it?" Melissa asked.

"Trust me," Jessica responded. "They made a mistake. A big one."

The warning bell sounded. Elizabeth glanced at her watch. "If I don't hurry, I'll be late to math," she said. "And don't worry about SOAR!, Jess. You'll probably like it."

"No, I won't," Jessica replied. "Because I'm getting out of SOAR! if it's the last thing I do. And *nobody* is going to change my mind."

"Wait up, Amy!" Elizabeth called as she dashed down the hallway and fell into step beside her friend. "You ran off after homeroom so quickly, I couldn't find you!"

"Ms. Wyler's giving us a quiz on fractions today," Amy said quietly. "I wanted to do a little last-minute cramming." She glanced at Elizabeth, then dropped her gaze to the floor. "Congratulations on getting into SOAR!."

"Thanks." Elizabeth paused outside the classroom door. "Amy, could we talk for a second?"

"I've really got to study, Elizabeth."

"I just—" Elizabeth hesitated. "I just wanted to tell you that I really think it's unfair you didn't get into SOAR!."

Amy shrugged. "It's no big deal."

"But I know how much you love science," Elizabeth said. "You got an A-plus on your last science project. And you placed second in the science fair. Besides," she added softly, "it just won't be as much fun without you."

"You'll have Jessica," Amy said dryly.

Elizabeth laughed. "She's convinced they made a mistake grading the tests."

Amy shifted her backpack from one shoulder to the other. "Maybe Jessica's right. Why would someone like her make it into SOAR!, when other people who actually *like* science . . ." Her voice trailed off.

"Maybe you'll get in next year, Amy," Elizabeth said gently.

Amy shook her head so hard that her thin blond hair fell into her face. She brushed it back impatiently. "It's my own fault, Elizabeth. You know I've never been very good at taking standardized tests."

"But you're a whiz at essay exams," Elizabeth pointed out.

Amy smiled, but her pale blue eyes were shiny with tears. "Like I said, it's no big deal. I'm going to be pretty busy for the next week or so anyway. I have to work out a new baton routine for the district basketball game. I'm trying this new move, but I'm not sure I'll have the nerve to do it by then."

"How come?"

"I only catch it about half the time," she admitted. "I do a really high toss, about twenty feet or so, and then I do a triple turn before catching it."

"Sounds great!" Elizabeth said.

"It is, when it works." Amy sighed and closed her eyes. "I don't know. Maybe I shouldn't even be doing a baton solo. It will probably be a total failure."

"No, it won't!" Elizabeth protested. "You're a great twirler."

"I don't know," Amy said quietly. "I used to think I was pretty good, but maybe I've just been fooling myself."

"Don't be so down on yourself, Amy," Elizabeth urged.

Amy nodded toward the door. "If I don't go in there and start cramming right now, I'm going to be even more down on myself when I flunk Ms. Wyler's quiz."

Maybe this new science program isn't going to be so much fun after all, Elizabeth thought as she followed Amy into class. SOAR! was already making Jessica and Amy miserable, and it hadn't even started yet.

Three

"What's wrong, Jessica?" Janet Howell asked that afternoon at the start of Boosters practice. "Are you still upset about the SOAR! test?"

Jessica was sitting in the bleachers, her head buried in her hands. She gave a little nod.

"I knew you had to be really upset when you didn't eat anything at lunch," Janet said. "Usually nobody eats more than you do."

"Thanks, Janet," Jessica murmured. It was good to have such understanding friends at a time like this.

"Did you talk to your science teacher?" Janet asked. She sat down next to Jessica and began filing her nails.

"Oh, I talked to him, all right."

Tamara Chase stepped into the gym. "Hey, Jess," she called. "What did Mr. Seigel say?"

Jessica sighed. "He said there's no way someone made a mistake grading my test."

"How can he be so sure?" Janet demanded. "Teachers make mistakes all the time."

"Computers don't," Jessica replied.

"Those tests were graded by a computer?" Tamara asked, surprised. "I guess that's why we had to fill in those little dots."

Lila was stretching out on a mat in the center of the gym. "I guess that means you really *are* a geek, Jess!" she joked.

Jessica glared at her. "Not funny, Lila."

Winston, who had been practicing back handsprings nearby, walked over to Jessica. "You know," he told her, "not everyone who made it into SOAR! is what you call a geek."

"Name someone," Janet challenged him.

"Well, *moi*, for starters," he said. "Or how about Todd Wilkins, or Elizabeth Wakefield, or Denny Jacobson?"

Jessica looked over at Janet in surprise. "*Denny's* going to be in SOAR!?"

"Denny's the exception that proves the rule," Janet said quickly. She smiled uneasily. "I have to admit, it shocked me a little at first, too. Then I realized that it's OK for guys to like science. But girls? I mean, give me a break! Can you name me one female scientist?"

Nobody answered.

"Can you name one *male* scientist?" Winston shot back.

Nobody answered.

"Don't you think you're being a little sexist, Janet?" Winston asked.

"Me? Sexist?" Janet cried. "I let you join the Boosters, didn't I?"

"Not without a fight," Winston reminded her.

"Janet's right, Winston," Jessica said. "Girls and science just don't mix. And even if there *are* one or two normal kids like Denny in SOAR!, that doesn't help me any. I have my reputation as a Unicorn to consider."

"You have *our* reputations to consider, too," Janet said, shaking her nail file at Jessica.

"What about me?" Winston asked. "I'm in SOAR! and I'm a member of the Boosters. Why aren't you worried about me ruining your reputations?"

"You've *already* ruined our reputations, Winston," Janet joked.

She stood up and stretched. "I guess we should get started," she said. "I want to get a special routine ready for the district basketball playoffs. We only have one week, you know."

"Amy's not here yet," Winston pointed out.

Janet groaned. "She's supposed to be putting together a solo baton routine. You'd think she could at least bother to show up for practice on time."

"I don't think she was feeling very well today," said Grace Oliver, a petite sixth grader who was dating Winston. "She was awfully quiet during gym class."

"Well, we'll just have to start without her," Janet said, looking annoyed. "Come on, guys, get your rears in gear."

Everyone headed for the center of the gym except for Jessica. "I'm going to sit this one out, Janet," she said. "I'm just not in the mood."

"Jessica has dweebitis," Winston exclaimed.

"Not for long," Janet said. She marched over, grabbed Jessica's hand, and yanked her off the bleachers. "Listen, Jess," she said. "We're all in this together. And we're going to find a way to save you from SOAR!, I promise."

For the first time all day, Jessica felt a little glimmer of hope. "Do you really think we can find a way to get me out of it?"

"Hey, we're Unicorns, aren't we?" Janet asked. "We always think of something."

"Uh-oh," Winston said, rolling his eyes. "Now you're *really* in trouble, Jessica!"

*   *   *

"We have some big news," Elizabeth announced at the dinner table that night.

"Hand me the salt, would you, Elizabeth?" Jessica said loudly.

"What kind of news?" asked Mr. Wakefield, helping himself to some salad.

Elizabeth smiled. "Maybe I should let Jessica tell you about it."

"The *salt*, Elizabeth," Jessica repeated urgently.

"It's right in front of you," said Steven, the twins' fourteen-year-old brother.

"Oh," Jessica said quietly. "Sorry."

"Maybe you should start wearing glasses again," Steven teased.

"So tell us your news," Mrs. Wakefield said, looking at Jessica expectantly.

"Elizabeth, could I see you in the kitchen for a minute?" Jessica asked, sending her twin a desperate look.

Elizabeth reached for her glass of milk. "Just let me tell everybody about SOAR! first."

Jessica gave Elizabeth a swift kick under the table.

"Ow!" Steven cried, reaching down to rub his shin. "One lousy joke about your glasses, and you permanently cripple me."

"Oh," Jessica said again. "Sorry."

"With a kick like that, you should try out for

the soccer team," Steven said. "The *boys'* soccer team."

"So anyway," Elizabeth said. "Do you want to tell them, Jess, or should I?"

"I really think we should wait, Elizabeth," Jessica replied, glaring at her sister. "You know—until we're sure."

"But we *are* sure."

"Will you tell us already?" Steven demanded. "The suspense is killing me."

Elizabeth grinned. "Jessica and I have been accepted into the SOAR! program at school!"

Jessica stared dejectedly at her mashed potatoes. Her life was officially ruined. Now that her parents knew about SOAR!, she'd never be able to get out of it.

"Soar program?" Steven repeated. "You're taking flying lessons?"

Mrs. Wakefield smiled broadly. "I am so proud of you both!" she exclaimed.

"How come they get to take flying lessons in middle school?" Steven cried.

"SOAR! is a special two-week science program, Steven," Mrs. Wakefield explained. "I got a notice about it from Mr. Clark, the middle school principal."

"Congratulations, girls," Mr. Wakefield said. "The program sounds like a great opportunity."

Steven reached for a roll. "I can't believe you two got into this science thing," he said, frowning. "Everybody knows girls are rotten at science."

"Steven!" Mrs. Wakefield cried. "I'm surprised at you! Where would you get an idea like that?"

"Really, Steven," Elizabeth said, rolling her eyes. "What a sexist thing to say."

"Not sexist," Steven corrected. "Accurate."

Mr. Wakefield leaned back in his chair, his arms crossed over his chest. "Would you mind explaining yourself, Steven?" he asked. "I'd love to hear your evidence."

Steven pointed to the twins. "There's your evidence, right in front of you. Most of the girls I know say they hate science."

"I don't," Elizabeth said proudly.

"Just you wait," Steven told her. "The first time the teacher asks you to cut up a worm, you'll squeal and quit. I guarantee it."

"Just wait and see!" Elizabeth cried, her eyes flashing angrily. "No way will we quit. Right, Jess?"

Jessica didn't answer. This probably wasn't the best time to admit that she was desperately trying to figure out a way to quit SOAR! before the program even started.

"It's nothing to feel bad about," Steven said with a cocky grin. "Guys are just naturally superior at some things. Right, Dad?"

"Don't go dragging me into this one, Steven," Mr. Wakefield said, shaking his head. "You're on your own."

"Take, for example, Ping-Pong," Steven continued.

"We'd play better if you didn't hog the Ping-Pong table all the time," Jessica shot back.

"I'm almost sorry I went to that garage sale last week," Mrs. Wakefield said. "Ever since I brought that table home, you kids haven't stopped fighting over it."

"Steven never lets us play," Jessica complained.

"It's wasted on amateurs like you," Steven said. "But I'll tell you what. After dinner, I'll allow you the honor of playing a game with me."

"Lucky us," Elizabeth said. "Pinch me, Jess. Am I dreaming?"

"Come on," Steven urged. "I'm getting tired of knocking the ball against the wall, and Dad won't play with me anymore."

"Sorry, Steven," Mr. Wakefield said, rubbing his left arm. "I think I'm getting Ping-Pong elbow."

"I'd like to play, Steven," Elizabeth said with

a sweet smile, "but you know how I am. I'll just squeal and quit."

"Jess?" Steven asked hopefully.

"You wouldn't want to play with a mere girl, Steven," Jessica said. "What fun would that be?"

"Mom?" Steven tried.

"I'd like to, Steven," she responded. "But I'm just not tough enough to be a Ping-Pong player."

"All right!" Steven held up his hands. "I get the message. But you're missing the chance of a lifetime."

"Sorry, Steven," Jessica said. "We've got more important things to do." She stood up and reached for her plate. "Come on, Lizzie," she said defiantly. "Let's go cut up some worms or something."

Four

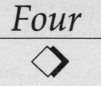

"You're late, Jessica," Mrs. Arnette said the next day as Jessica tried to slip into social studies class unnoticed.

Jessica pointed to the clock behind Mrs. Arnette's desk. "Come on, I'm only two seconds late," she said. "Nobody gives a detention for two lousy seconds."

"I do," Mrs. Arnette replied. She filled out another yellow slip and handed it to Jessica.

Jessica walked down the aisle and flopped into her chair. "She enjoys making me suffer," she muttered under her breath.

"Mrs. Arnette?" An eighth-grade boy eased open the door and handed the teacher a sheet of paper.

"Thank you," Mrs. Arnette said. She scanned

the note. "This is a list of the students who will be missing class beginning on Monday while they participate in the SOAR! program," she explained. "Hmm. Elizabeth, Todd, Julie," she read. "It's nice to see so many names—" Suddenly she stopped and looked up in surprise. "Jessica?" she cried. "The office must have made some kind of mistake! Or are there *two* Jessica Wakefields in the school?"

Everyone burst into laughter. Jessica felt her cheeks burn. But what could she say? Mrs. Arnette was right—she wasn't the SOAR! type, and everyone knew it. Still, it was pretty humiliating to be made fun of by her own teacher!

Jessica sat through the rest of the period fuming over the way Mrs. Arnette had teased her in front of the whole class. When the bell rang, she was the first one out of her seat and through the door.

Elizabeth and Amy caught up with Jessica in the hall a few seconds later. "I couldn't believe what Mrs. Arnette said to you, Jess," Elizabeth said sympathetically.

"Me neither," Jessica replied. "The worst thing is, I don't even *want* to be in SOAR!." She shrugged. "Of course, after you blew it last night by telling Mom and Dad, I don't know how I'll ever get out of it."

"I told you I was sorry," Elizabeth said. "How was I supposed to know you wanted to keep it a secret?"

"I don't see why you're making such a big deal out of this, Jessica," Amy said quietly. "A lot of people think you're lucky to have gotten in."

"Lucky?" Jessica repeated in disbelief. "If you think I'm so lucky, maybe you should take my place, Amy."

"Me?" Amy said. "Why would I want to be in SOAR!? It sounds incredibly boring. That's probably what they ought to call it—BORE."

"Tell me about it," Jessica agreed. "It's especially awful for someone like me. I have my reputation to consider, after all. If I end up having to take that stupid class, the Unicorns will be publicly humiliated. It's not good for our image."

"I would think the Unicorns would be proud to have a member in SOAR!," Elizabeth argued. She paused. "At least, they *should* be proud."

Amy laughed scornfully. "What planet did you just step off of, Elizabeth? Since when do the Unicorns care about school?"

"We do so care about school!" Jessica protested. "School spirit, school lunches . . ."

"But not school *work*," Elizabeth said. "That's why Mrs. Arnette and Steven were so surprised to hear that you're in SOAR!, Jess."

"Who knows what's going on in their de-
mented brains?" Jessica snapped. But she knew
what Elizabeth meant. Mrs. Arnette thought Jessica was too irresponsible to be in a program like
SOAR!. And Steven thought she was too *female*.

"Don't you want to prove they're wrong
about you?" Elizabeth asked.

Jessica hesitated. "Well, they *are* wrong if
they think I couldn't handle a class like SOAR!,"
she said. "I mean, just because I get a few detentions now and then doesn't mean I couldn't handle a stupid science course." She paused and
thought for a moment. "Well, OK, I have more
than a *few* detentions."

"You have enough yellow slips to wallpaper
your whole locker," Amy pointed out.

"But just because I could do OK in SOAR!
doesn't mean I actually want to be in it," Jessica
continued firmly. "I could do OK in the Chess
Club, too, if I really felt like being a geek."

"But Jess—" Elizabeth began.

"The point *is*, I'm a Unicorn, not a geek,"
Jessica said. "And that's not going to change."

"Jessica, I've been trying to think of ways to
get you out of SOAR!," Ellen said that afternoon in
the girls' bathroom between fifth and sixth periods.

"Any ideas?" Jessica asked. "I'm desperate!"

"I think you should transfer to another school for two weeks," Ellen replied.

"Dumb idea, Ellen," Janet pronounced as she ran a comb through her hair. "Very dumb."

"How about if you pretend you're sick for two weeks?" Lila suggested.

"I could never fake my mom out that long," Jessica replied. She gazed into the mirror and puckered her lips. "She knows all my tricks."

"What's that lip gloss you're using, Jess?" Mandy asked.

"It's called Magic Mud," Jessica explained. "It's part of the new Earth Tones line." She dabbed a few spots of color on her lower lip and spread them with her pinkie finger. "It contains genuine mud. And it's a blusher, lip gloss, and eye shadow, all in one."

"Maybe it's the lighting in here," Mandy said with a smile, "but it looks awfully brown to me."

"Why don't you just go out in your back yard and eat a little dirt?" Ellen teased. "You'd get the same effect for free!"

Jessica rolled her eyes at Ellen and carefully stroked some of the Magic Mud onto her cheeks. "So does anyone else have any brilliant plans for getting me out of SOAR!?" she asked.

"We're working on it, Jessica," Janet assured her as the warning bell rang. "Don't worry."

"Easy for you to say," Jessica muttered.

"Come on, Jess," Mandy urged. "You'd better hurry, or you'll be late to science class."

"And we all know how much you love science," Lila teased.

"Can it, Lila," Jessica snapped. She stared into the mirror and tried to smile. Her cheeks felt a little strange. "Go ahead," she told her friends. "I just want to experiment with my mud for another minute."

When the bathroom had emptied out, Jessica rubbed her face. The Magic Mud seemed to be turning into Magic Cement. Her cheeks were the color and texture of brownies.

"Great. Just great," Jessica moaned as the final bell rang. Frantically she began to wash the mud off her face. She was already going to be late. There was no point in being late *and* humiliated.

When she was finished, Jessica dried her face with a paper towel and sighed. So much for Magic Mud.

She was definitely not having a good week.

That evening, Jessica was watching TV in the family room when she heard a muffled groan. She reached for the remote control and switched off the sound.

A moment later she heard the sound again. It seemed to be coming from right below her.

"Did you hear that?" she asked Elizabeth, who was curled up in an easy chair reading a mystery.

"Hear what?" Elizabeth asked.

"A groan or something. It sounded like it was coming from the basement."

"Oh, I think Steven is down there playing Ping-Pong," Elizabeth said, her eyes still glued to her book.

"Oh, *man!*" shouted someone from the basement.

"You must have heard that," Jessica said.

"That's Steven, all right," Elizabeth remarked.

"Who's he playing against?"

"Cathy," Elizabeth said. "She came over a while ago, and Steven started bugging her to play him." Cathy Connors was Steven's girlfriend.

"Oh." Jessica picked up the remote control and turned the sound back on. Suddenly Jessica clicked the sound off again. "Wait a minute. You don't think she's winning, do you?"

Elizabeth looked up from her book and her eyes met Jessica's. Without another word, both girls jumped up and dashed for the basement door.

They arrived at the bottom of the dusty

wooden steps just in time to see a Ping-Pong ball go sailing over Steven's shoulder. Steven's paddle had missed it by at least two inches.

"I just missed it!" Steven groaned.

"I'm sorry," Cathy said with a shrug. "Would you like to quit now? This is really a pretty dumb game."

"Oh, you'd like me to quit while you're ahead, wouldn't you?" Steven said accusingly.

"Cathy's ahead?" Elizabeth asked in amazement.

"The mighty macho man is losing to a *girl*?" Jessica crowed.

"I'm only ahead by a few points," Cathy said.

"How few?" Jessica demanded.

"What's the score now?" Cathy asked Steven. "I can never remember it."

Steven mumbled something.

"What was that, Steven?" Elizabeth asked.

"I said she's ahead by twelve points! All right?" Steven exploded.

For a moment, Jessica almost felt sorry for her brother. "I guess you've probably played a lot, huh?" she asked Cathy.

"Not really," Cathy said. "This is my first game."

"Don't you two have some kind of science dweebette work to do?" Steven demanded. "You're spoiling my concentration." He served the ball with lightning speed, but Cathy moved even faster and sent the ball flying back over Steven's shoulder.

"Oh, no, Steven," Jessica said. "We leave all that science stuff to the big strong boys."

"Really," Elizabeth agreed. "You know how lousy we girls are at things like science, and math . . ."

". . . and Ping-Pong," Jessica added with a laugh. It seemed like the first time she'd laughed all day.

Five

◇

"So where are the desks for this stupid class?" Jessica demanded on Monday morning. "And where's the teacher?"

"Maybe since it's a new class, they had to order extra desks," Elizabeth suggested.

Jessica gazed around the room. She recognized most of the students, although there were some eighth graders whose names she didn't know. A few of the students were examining a strange assortment of tools, test tubes, and batteries spread around on several long tables. There were tall stools scattered around the room, along with wooden boxes, a large plastic skeleton, an old beat-up bicycle, several children's toys, and a tall steel ladder.

"This is the weirdest classroom I've ever seen," Todd remarked.

"Maybe the teacher forgot to come," Jessica said hopefully.

"Ta-ta-ta taaaaa!"

Jessica and Elizabeth both jumped.

"Ta-ta-ta taaaa! Your attention, please!"

Through the open doorway came a strange silver machine, about two feet tall. It had two big red lightbulbs for eyes, and it moved on tracks like a tank.

"It's a robot!" Elizabeth exclaimed.

"Your attention, please! Get ready to SOAR!, people!" the robot continued in its shrill voice. "Presenting, for your learning pleasure, the one and only Mr. Baker!"

Following the robot was one of the oddest-looking men Jessica had ever seen. He was even older than Mrs. Arnette, but he was wearing sky blue high-top sneakers and a matching tie painted with pictures of fluffy white clouds. He had wild silvery gray hair, and deep blue eyes magnified by thick red-framed glasses. Mr. Baker was definitely not dressed like your average, everyday teacher.

"No time for long introductions," Mr. Baker began. "We have tons of stuff to do. Tons! Why, we have to uncover the secrets of the universe, and we only have an hour to do it!"

"Do you think maybe he's insane?" Jessica whispered to Elizabeth.

Mr. Baker pointed at the robot waiting silently by the door. "That's Tobor," he said.

"Robot spelled backwards," Jessica muttered under her breath. "How juvenile."

"Tobor talks if I tell him to, and he's programmed to use his laser to zap any student who tries to leave this room," Mr. Baker continued. "I am Mr. Baker, and—" He stopped suddenly and stared at Jessica, then at Elizabeth, then back at Jessica again. "Either you two are twins, or my eyes have crossed," he exclaimed.

"We're twins," Elizabeth said. "I'm Elizabeth, and this is Jessica."

"Twins! Perfect! Sit down, both of you."

"There aren't any desks," Jessica pointed out.

"True enough. We don't need desks, because we won't be doing much sitting." He pointed to Winston Egbert. "You, what's your name?"

"Um, Winston?" Winston answered nervously.

"Not sure, eh? Well, whoever you are, grab two of those stools and put them over by that ladder. Yes, right in front of it there. Good." Mr. Baker spun around and grabbed Lloyd by the shoulder. "Have you ever filled up a water balloon?"

"I guess so," Lloyd replied.

"Another one who's not sure," Mr. Baker said with a shrug. He pulled two balloons from his pocket. "Here. Run over to the sink and fill these up with water."

Lloyd grabbed the two balloons, but Mr. Baker gripped his shoulder. "Wait. Instructions. *Very* important. Fill the blue balloon full, but only fill the red balloon a little bit. Blue big, red little. Blue big, red little. Blue little, red big. Got it? Blue red, little big. Now go. We have to hurry. We have science to do."

Lloyd nodded doubtfully as some of the kids laughed.

"Now, my two twins," Mr. Baker said, rubbing his hands together. "You'll find a couple of raincoats in that wooden box over there. Put them on, then come and sit side by side on these two stools."

Jessica stole a glance at Elizabeth. Maybe her sister understood what this was all about. After all, Elizabeth *liked* science. But Elizabeth looked as mystified as Jessica felt.

The girls put on the bright yellow raincoats and sat down on the stools. Around the room, students were whispering and laughing.

"I feel like a complete dweeb," Jessica whispered to Elizabeth.

Lloyd handed Mr. Baker the water balloons. Mr. Baker slowly climbed up the steel ladder behind Jessica and Elizabeth.

Jessica had a very bad feeling about what was coming next.

"My question is this," Mr. Baker announced. "If I drop both of these balloons—the big one and the small one—at exactly the same time, which twin will get wet first?"

Jessica looked up to see the big blue balloon poised several feet above her head. "You can't drop that on me!" she wailed. "I'll get wet."

"Of course you'll get wet," Mr. Baker said calmly. "That's not the question. The question is, who will get wet *first*—you, or your sister?"

"I'll get wet first, of course," Jessica replied. "My balloon's three times as big."

"So, you believe that the bigger, heavier balloon will fall faster than the smaller, lighter balloon."

"Of course!"

"So that would be your *hypothesis*. Your *hypothesis* is that heavier things fall faster, right?"

"I guess so," Jessica said, eyeing the balloon warily. "Now can I get up?"

"But a *hypothesis* is just a guess. We don't

know if your *hypothesis* is correct," Mr. Baker said in a regretful tone. "A *hypothesis* must be tested before we can know if it's correct."

"But I don't care if it's correct," Jessica moaned.

"How about if I told you that if your hypothesis is correct, I will let you wear this?" Mr. Baker reached inside his jacket and pulled out a crumpled green cap. Embroidered on the front in white letters were the words *SOAR! Superstar.*

"Um, no thanks," Jessica said, trying to sound polite. *Give it to one of the science nerds*, she added to herself.

"Hmmm. Well, the cap only goes to a student who is particularly bright on a given day," Mr. Baker said. He stared at Jessica for a moment, tapping his finger on his chin. "What about if I say that if your *hypothesis* is correct, I'll give you an A for the whole course and let you go home?"

Jessica started to protest, but suddenly she realized what Mr. Baker was offering her. All she had to do was suffer one little water balloon, and all her problems would be over.

"Shall we test your hypothesis?" Mr. Baker asked.

Jessica shrugged. "All right." She pulled the hood of the raincoat up over her head.

"Class," Mr. Baker said from atop the ladder,

"Jessica has put forward a *hypothesis*. We must test that *hypothesis* by performing an *experiment*. Everyone! Eyes on the balloons."

Jessica could see that everyone was staring at Mr. Baker. An instant later she felt a wet explosion on her head.

The hood kept most of her hair dry, but her face was soaked. She wiped the water out of her eyes and looked over at Elizabeth. Elizabeth's much smaller balloon had barely made a splash.

"Now do I get my A?" Jessica demanded as she stood up and started taking off her raincoat.

Mr. Baker climbed down the ladder. "Class?" he asked.

"No way," Denny said, shaking his head. "Both the balloons landed at the same time."

"Same time," Winston Egbert agreed, nodding.

"But that's impossible," Jessica protested.

"Jessica," Mr. Baker said. "We have performed an experiment to test your *hypothesis*, and your *hypothesis* was wrong." He smiled at the twins. "Luckily it's pretty warm in here, so you girls should dry out in a few minutes."

"Luckily," Jessica muttered.

Mr. Baker turned to the class. "The human race has been around for millions of years. And for almost that whole time everyone assumed that heavy things fall faster than light things. It wasn't until about four hundred years ago that a guy named Galileo decided to test the *hypothesis*."

"He dropped water balloons on people's heads?" Jessica asked.

"Actually, he dropped cannonballs off a tower. But what was true then is true today. Everything falls at the same speed unless there's a difference in air resistance. And the moral is—never assume anything. Nothing is true until it has been proved." He bowed to the twins. "Thank you, ladies, for helping us all understand the universe a little better."

"Any time," Jessica muttered, but at the sight of Mr. Baker's wide grin, she couldn't help smiling back, just a little.

"So how was it?" Janet demanded as Jessica took her seat at the Unicorner that day at lunch.

"Tell us all the awful details," Ellen urged sympathetically.

Jessica poked at the brown lump of meat loaf in the middle of her plate. She really didn't want to talk about her first morning of SOAR!. After all, they expected her to tell them horror stories about being trapped in Loserland. And the awful, embarrassing truth was, she hadn't minded it nearly as much as she'd thought she would. Sure, Mr. Baker was a very strange man. And most of the kids were pretty strange, too. She'd never seen so many pocket protectors in one room. But when they'd all been laughing at Mr. Baker's crazy antics, she'd almost forgotten about all that. She'd even lent Cammi Adams her favorite purple pen.

"So?" Janet prompted.

Jessica looked up, startled. "Sorry," she mumbled. "I was just wondering what kind of meat they put in this meat loaf."

"Who says it's meat?" Lila joked. "Maybe it's just an amazing simulation."

Ellen laughed. "Or somebody's science fair project."

Belinda took a bite of her meat loaf, then spat it out into her napkin. "Yuck!" she cried. "I think this is a case for your SOAR! class, Jess. Why don't you take a sample of this stuff back to class and put it under the microscope? It may actually be hazardous to our health."

"So tell us about SOAR!, Jessica," Mandy said as she joined the group. As usual, Mandy was dressed in a style all her own. Today she was wearing bright blue leggings, a black miniskirt, a pair of unlaced black high-tops, and a bright blue oversize T-shirt with a silkscreened picture of a baby panda on the front.

"Nice outfit, Mandy," Jessica commented.

Mandy bought her clothes at flea markets and secondhand shops, but somehow the finished look was always something special. She was really unique, Jessica thought, just like the rest of her friends in the Unicorns. Suddenly her mind flashed to an image of Cammi Adams, with her runny nose and her monogrammed calculator. *What came over me this morning?* Jessica wondered uneasily. What was she, anyway—a Unicorn, or a dweeb?

Mandy covered her meat loaf with her napkin. "Somebody needs to give this stuff a decent burial," she commented. She nudged Jessica with her elbow. "So? What did you guys do this morning? Build a nuclear reactor, maybe?"

"That's this afternoon," Jessica replied. "This morning we came up with a cure for the common cold."

Mandy grinned. "Well, don't be discouraged. It's only natural you'd get off to a slow start. This is just your first day, after all."

"What's the teacher like?" Belinda asked.

Jessica shrugged. "Weird," she said. "He has this little robot with him that tells you when you've given a dumb answer."

Lila rolled her eyes. "How juvenile."

Jessica nodded. "Mr. Baker dropped water balloons on Elizabeth and me," she added casually.

"Are you kidding?" Lila asked.

"Nope. We were wearing raincoats, fortunately."

"Poor Jessica," Ellen said sympathetically. "Stranded with an insane teacher and all those geeks for two whole weeks."

"They're not *all* geeks," Janet reminded Ellen. "Denny's in there, don't forget."

"But he's the exception that proves the rule, right?" Ellen asked, repeating Janet's words.

Janet smiled with satisfaction. "Exactly." She leaned across the table. "So did Denny say anything interesting, Jessica?" she asked.

"Interesting?"

"Like, did he mention me?"

"He was standing on the other side of the room, Janet. I don't think he even knows who I am."

"He's adorable, isn't he?"

"I didn't really notice, Janet. I was busy getting water balloons dropped on me, remember?" Jessica let out a long sigh. "So, has anybody come up with a solution to my problem yet?" she asked. "There's got to be a way out of this."

"Anybody come up with anything?" Janet asked.

Everybody shook their heads.

"Maybe you should just stick it out," suggested Mary Wallace, a seventh grader who was treasurer of the Unicorns. She smiled. "Who knows? You might even learn something interesting, Jess."

"*Learn* something?" Janet repeated. "Are you insane, Mary? Who cares if Jessica *learns* anything? She's got to get out of that geek asylum. That's all there is to it."

"You just hang in there a little longer, Jessica," Ellen said, patting her on the shoulder. "Work on your nuclear reactor or whatever, and maybe by tomorrow we'll have an answer."

"Hey, Jess!"

Jessica twisted around in her seat to see Aaron Dallas walking over. Aaron was one of the cutest guys in the sixth grade and her sort-of boyfriend. She wondered whether he'd heard about SOAR! yet. Would he even want to be seen with her once he knew?

Aaron paused at the end of the table. "I guess I should say congratulations," he said, smiling at Jessica.

"Congratulations?" she repeated.

"You know—about SOAR!."

Jessica wasn't sure what to say. Was Aaron making fun of her? She couldn't tell. "Well, you know, I sort of freaked when I found out," she said.

"Me too! I mean, you're not exactly the science whiz type, you know?" He ran his fingers through his hair. "Of course, I didn't think you were exactly the basketball type either, and it turned out you know almost as much about it as I do."

"More," Jessica teased.

"Hey, I wouldn't go *that* far," Aaron said with a laugh. He nodded toward the cafeteria door. "Well, I guess I should get going. Jake and Bruce and I are going to go shoot a few baskets."

"Bye," Jessica said, flashing him her best smile, complete with dimple.

"Big no-no, Jess," Janet said as soon as Aaron was gone.

"What?" Jessica asked in surprise.

"*Never* tell a guy you're better at something than he is!" Janet cried. "Every girl knows that."

"I was just kidding," Jessica protested. "Besides, I *do* know as much as Aaron does about basketball. Maybe even more!"

"But you should never let a guy know you know more," Ellen told her.

Jessica crossed her arms over her chest. "Why not? One of the reasons Aaron likes me is because I know a lot about basketball."

Lila rolled her eyes. "Look, Jess. Guys have fragile egos. They need to think they're superior, so we girls let them believe it."

"The point is, Jessica, you can't let Aaron know you're better than he is, or it will ruin your relationship." Janet said firmly. "That's why this SOAR! thing is so dangerous!"

"But Aaron congratulated me," Jessica pointed out.

Janet and Lila exchanged a knowing look. "He was just being sarcastic," Janet explained.

"I don't think so," Mandy said. "I think he really meant it."

"Well, you can listen to Mandy if you want, Jess," Janet said. "But I have far more experience with guys, and I say they don't like girls who are smarter than they are. After all, did Aaron get into SOAR!?"

"Well, no—"

"So how do you think that makes him feel?"

"I don't know. How do *you* feel? Denny got in and you didn't."

Janet groaned. "That's different, because I'm the girl and he's the guy."

"This discussion is ridiculous!" Mary exclaimed. "Janet, I can't believe you're actually telling Jessica to act stupid for the sake of a guy."

"*And* for the sake of our reputations," Lila added.

"It's not so hard to act dumb, Jess," Ellen advised.

"I wish I'd never taken that test," Jessica said sadly. "I could have gone my whole life without knowing I was smart." She sighed. "All I know is, I was a whole lot happier when I was dumb."

Six

◇

"No, not Mars. I told you, I'm from Venus. I don't even *like* people from Mars," Mr. Baker said. He was pacing back and forth in front of the class, wearing a pair of pointed plastic ears and some fake antennae.

It was Tuesday morning. The SOAR! students were spread around the room, sitting on the floor or perched on tables.

"OK, first of all," Denny said, "there's no life on Venus. So no matter what you say, you couldn't be from Venus."

"How do you know for sure?" Mr. Baker asked.

"Spacecraft have visited Venus, and they never saw anything that looked alive," Denny said reasonably.

"But the spacecraft only looked at a small part of the planet," Nora Mercandy said.

"That's right," Elizabeth agreed. "I checked in our encyclopedia at home last night. All they really did was take photographs. Maybe they looked in the wrong places. I mean, what if a spacecraft from Venus came to Earth and only took pictures of the north pole? They wouldn't think anybody lived here, either."

"Still," Denny argued, "Venus is not the kind of place where living things would hang out. For one thing, it's too hot. I checked in my almanac, and it says the surface of Venus is about nine hundred degrees."

Jessica considered this. Maybe Denny was right. Obviously, that was much too hot for any normal life. "Maybe everybody on Venus lives in caves, or places where they can keep the heat out," she suggested.

"You mean everybody on Venus lives in air-conditioned houses?" Mr. Baker asked, laughing.

Normally, Jessica would have hated having a teacher laugh at her idea, but with Mr. Baker it was different. He wasn't really laughing *at* her. He just thought her idea was funny.

"Maybe so," Jessica said. "Maybe they all have really advanced air-conditioning systems."

"All right, Jessica," Mr. Baker responded.

"Maybe they do. But they couldn't always have had air conditioning. How did they survive in the years before some smart Venusian invented the first air conditioner?"

Jessica thought for a moment. Mr. Baker had her there. She was being dumb. But then an idea struck her. "Wait a minute. How do we know it was always so hot on Venus? Maybe it used to be cool, but then it got hotter and hotter for thousands of years, so the Venusians had time to get used to it and come up with air conditioning."

As soon as the words were out of her mouth, she felt her cheeks begin to burn. She felt very self-conscious, talking this way in class. She *never* participated in Mr. Seigel's science class. Sometimes she even slept.

"Very, very good, Jessica." Mr. Baker walked over to Cammi and pulled the SOAR! cap off her head. "Sorry, Cammi," he said, "but you've had it for a day already, and Jessica has just made a very good point."

Mr. Baker dropped the cap onto Jessica's head. Jessica glanced around anxiously to see if anyone was laughing at her. But all she saw were envious looks on most of her classmates' faces.

"You see," Mr. Baker said, "sometimes conditions on a planet change. They've changed many times right here on Earth. Venus is so hot because of something called the greenhouse effect. If you have too much carbon dioxide in the atmosphere, it traps the heat from the sun and turns a planet into an oven. And here's something to think about: we may be seeing the beginning of our own greenhouse effect right here on Earth."

The bell rang, and Mr. Baker began shooing the students out of the room. "Class is over," he cried. "All done. Go home, go home."

But most of the students lingered. "What do you mean it might be happening here?" Elizabeth asked.

"Do you really think the Earth could end up being as hot as Venus?" Denny demanded.

Jessica picked up her backpack and started to leave, but as she reached the door, she paused for a moment to hear Mr. Baker's answer.

Mr. Baker shrugged. "It's possible. Every year we cut down more and more of our forests, and it's trees that take carbon dioxide and turn it into oxygen."

"So where does the carbon dioxide come from?" Elizabeth asked.

"Breathe out," Mr. Baker instructed.

"What?" Elizabeth looked puzzled.

"Breathe out. You see, there are a lot of things that make carbon dioxide. Automobiles, factories, fires. And you, every time you breathe out."

"But—" Jessica began, taking a step back into the room.

"Ah, ah," Mr. Baker said, holding up his hand. "I have a meeting with the principal. I promise we'll talk more about the greenhouse effect tomorrow. And Venus, and anything else you'd like. But right now it's getting late, and—"

"Oh, my gosh!" Jessica shouted. "The Unicorns!"

"All right," Mr. Baker said doubtfully. "If you want, we can talk about unicorns tomorrow, too."

"I have a Unicorn meeting, and I'm late," Jessica cried. "They're going to kill me!" She dashed out of the room.

"Mousse, mousse, mousse!" Janet said firmly to Lila. "Nothing works better than Mega Mousse."

Jessica stood in the doorway of Janet's bedroom, trying to catch her breath. Janet, Ellen, and Lila were sitting on the bed arguing. The rest of the Unicorns were lounging around on the carpet looking bored.

"Super Spray is better. You're just mad because I'm the one who discovered it," Lila said, crossing her arms over her chest.

"Sorry I'm late," Jessica interrupted breathlessly.

The three girls stopped arguing and turned to stare at her. "We've been waiting for you, Jessica," Janet declared in her bossiest tone. "You know it's important for us to begin meetings exactly on time. You've already missed a very important debate."

"I'm sorry," Jessica said sincerely.

"Where were you?" Janet demanded.

"I . . . we were just talking about the greenhouse effect and Venus, and Mr. Baker sort of made us stay after class—"

"You're late for our meeting because you wanted to hang around with your nerd pals to talk about green grass on Venus?" Janet asked, rolling her eyes.

"There's grass on Venus?" Ellen asked.

"Jessica's talking about the greenhouse effect," Mandy said.

"Yeah," Belinda added. "Too many trees and forests are getting cut down, so the earth is—"

"Excuse me!" Janet exploded. "Is Jessica's nerd disease spreading? A minute ago we were talking about mousse!"

"And Super Spray," Lila added.

"What do *you* think, Jessica?" Janet asked. "Which one is better? Mega Mousse or Super Spray?"

"Well, I like Mega Mousse," Jessica said thoughtfully. "But you know how we could decide? We could compare them. You know—do an experiment."

"An experiment?" Janet repeated the word suspiciously. "Where did you get *that* idea?"

"From"—Jessica hesitated—"from *Chic* magazine," she said quickly. "It said you should always experiment with different beauty products."

Janet eyed her doubtfully.

"Really," Jessica said, but she had the feeling everyone was looking at her as if she were from another planet.

Probably Venus.

"Elizabeth, do you have any film in your camera?" Amy asked Wednesday afternoon. "Because we should definitely preserve this moment for posterity."

Elizabeth looked up from her SOAR! textbook. "What do you mean?"

"Look at the three of us," Amy said. She gestured toward Jessica, who was lying on Elizabeth's bedroom floor reading. "When was the last time Jessica actually studied with us?"

Elizabeth thought for a minute. "Come to think of it, I don't think Jessica has *ever* studied with us."

"Would you two cut it out?" Jessica demanded. "I feel weird enough as it is."

Elizabeth and Amy exchanged a smile. Elizabeth was happy she'd been able to talk her friend into coming over this afternoon. "I'm glad you came over, Amy," Elizabeth said.

Amy stretched out on Elizabeth's bed and yawned. "Me too," she said. "I feel like you've disappeared at school. Ever since SOAR! started, there are all these empty seats in every class. It's strange. And today you were even gone at lunch because of your field trip to the planetarium."

"I wish you could have come along," Elizabeth said. "Maybe we can all go again some weekend."

Amy looked down at her hands. "Maybe."

"Well, the good thing is, SOAR! won't last for too much longer," Elizabeth said.

"I've been pretty busy, anyway," Amy said as she rifled through the pages of her social studies book. "You know—with my baton routine and stuff."

"How's that going?" Elizabeth asked.

"OK, I guess. But I'm not sure it'll be ready in time for the game next week. I'm still having trouble catching the dumb thing. Maybe I should just forget about it."

"Amy, you can't do that!" Elizabeth exclaimed. "I'm sure it'll be great. Won't it, Jessica?"

"What?" Jessica asked distractedly, looking up from her book.

"Did you hear what Amy said?"

"Sorry," Jessica said. "I guess I was sort of involved in my reading."

Amy sat up abruptly. "That's OK, Jess," she said coolly. "I know how much you've always loved science." She reached for her book bag. "I've got to get going, anyway."

"But you just got here!" Elizabeth began.

"What's the point of studying together?" Amy said angrily. "We're not even in the same classes anymore."

Before Elizabeth could answer, Amy dashed out of the room and down the stairs. Elizabeth followed, trying desperately to think of something to say to make Amy feel better.

"See you, Elizabeth," Amy said shortly when she reached the Wakefields' front door. "In two more weeks."

"You know, Amy," Elizabeth said quickly, "there are a couple of homework projects I've got to work on for SOAR! that look like they're going to be tough. I was thinking maybe you could give me a hand with them, if you have time—"

"Why don't you ask Jessica?" Amy interrupted.

"Because you're so good at science."

"Not good enough."

"Just because you didn't do well—"

Amy reached for the doorknob. "I have to go."

"Amy, you know this SOAR! program is only for two weeks," Elizabeth said gently. "It'll be over soon and everything will go back to the way it was."

Amy's pale blue eyes were shiny with tears. "No, it won't, Elizabeth," she said. "It won't be the same at all." She yanked open the door. "Do me a favor, OK?"

"Anything."

"Don't bring up SOAR! anymore. I don't want to hear about it ever again."

Seven

Elizabeth walked slowly back up to her room. "I've never seen Amy so down," she said. She stepped over Jessica, who was still sprawled out on the floor.

"Hmm," Jessica mumbled.

"Jessica!" Elizabeth snapped, slumping into her desk chair. "Are you even listening?"

Jessica looked up, startled. "Sorry. Did you know that every single minute fifty-three acres of tropical rain forest are cut down?"

Elizabeth sighed. She knew she should be thrilled that her twin was finally showing an interest in her schoolwork, but right now she needed someone to talk to. "I'm worried about Amy, Jess," she said. "Did you hear what she said about her baton routine?"

"Not exactly."

"Well, she was wondering whether or not she should even perform at the district playoff game."

"She'd better," Jessica said. "The Boosters are counting on her."

"I think her confidence is a little shaky since she didn't get into SOAR!. You know how much Amy loves science."

"Too bad she can't take my place," Jessica said. "It would make life a lot easier."

"I thought you were enjoying SOAR!" Elizabeth exclaimed.

"I am, sort of. I mean I think I am. I mean—" Jessica groaned. "How should I know if I'm enjoying it? I'm not *used* to enjoying hard subjects, especially science. It feels—you know. Weird." She stared at Elizabeth doubtfully. "Is this how you feel about school all the time?"

Elizabeth laughed. "*Most* of the time. Ask me again when we're doing word problems in math, and I might give you a different answer."

Jessica sighed. "I feel so strange. Like I've been taken over by an alien being or something."

Elizabeth nodded understandingly. "It's sort of like if I suddenly decided I wanted to join the Unicorns, huh?"

"Exactly! And speaking of the Unicorns, you should have heard them yesterday when I was late to a meeting. Janet and Lila were furious. And Janet said I was betraying the Unicorn name."

"You're not betraying the Unicorns just because you like a science class," Elizabeth argued.

"Is that clock really right?" Jessica demanded suddenly, pointing to the alarm clock on Elizabeth's nightstand.

"Sure."

"It's quarter to *six*?" Jessica cried.

"What's the big deal?"

Jessica leaped up, tossing her SOAR! textbook onto Elizabeth's bed. "Lizzie, it's practically six o'clock, and the phone hasn't rung once! Not once!" Her eyes were wide with terror. "Do you realize what this means?"

"Well, um . . ."

"It means I'm a social outcast, Elizabeth! A washed-up nobody." Jessica flopped onto the bed dramatically. "It's finally happened, Elizabeth. I am now officially a nerd."

"Just because the phone hasn't rung?" Elizabeth asked, barely stifling a smile.

"You know why it hasn't rung?"

"I'm sure you're going to tell me."

"Because I've been reading a science book, that's why!" Jessica pulled a pillow over her head and moaned, then sat up and tossed the pillow across the room. "There's a direct scientific—what's that word Mr. Baker always uses? Coronation?"

"Correlation," Elizabeth said. "It means there's a connection."

"And there is," Jessica insisted. "Somehow the world knows when you're a nerd. People sense it. They know you're the kind of person who would bury herself in a book about the rain forest, so what do they do?"

Elizabeth raised an eyebrow. "What?"

"They stop calling you, that's what!" Jessica jumped to her feet. "I have to go call Lila before my reputation is completely destroyed."

"Is there anything I can do to help?" Elizabeth joked.

"Promise me you'll never breathe a word of this to anyone," Jessica whispered. "No one."

"Your secret's safe with me," Elizabeth promised.

Jessica ran into the hallway and began dialing the phone. "Hello, Lila?" Elizabeth heard her say.

Elizabeth got up and closed the door so she could concentrate on her reading, but a few minutes later Jessica exploded back into the room.

"Are you sure you want to hang out in a nerd bedroom?" Elizabeth teased.

"This SOAR! stuff is ruining me!" Jessica cried. "Do you know what today is?"

"The sixteenth?"

"No! I mean yes, but it's also Ellen's birthday! All the Unicorns gave her presents during lunch. And where was I? At the planetarium being a nerd! I would have completely forgotten if Lila hadn't just reminded me."

"I'm sure if you call Ellen she'll understand," Elizabeth suggested calmly.

"I did, right after I hung up with Lila. And do you know what Ellen said?"

Elizabeth shook her head.

"Ellen said she was too busy to talk because she couldn't wait to do her *science* homework."

"So?"

"So?" Jessica repeated in disbelief. "Ellen couldn't wait to do her *science* homework? The same Ellen who once tried to get out of a lab project on fruit flies by claiming she was allergic to bananas? *That* Ellen?" Jessica sat down on the edge of Elizabeth's bed, looking completely dejected. "She was making fun of me, Lizzie. Ellen Riteman was making fun of me. My life really *is* over."

*   *   *

"Friday night for sure. And trust me on this—you'll be sorry!" Steven yelled into the phone before hanging up.

"Sorry for what?" Elizabeth asked as she and Jessica walked into the kitchen.

"Sorry she agreed to go out with him, I'll bet," Jessica said.

"Do I eavesdrop on your private conversations?" Steven demanded.

"Yes!" the girls both exclaimed at once.

Steven opened the refrigerator door and gazed inside. "Well, since you're so interested, I'm happy to announce that Cathy has officially agreed to a Ping-Pong rematch."

"Good," Elizabeth said. "Now maybe we can get this thing settled once and for all."

Steven pulled out a carton of milk and a plate with half a chocolate cake on it. "I just want to set the record straight, that's all."

"What if it turns out that Cathy actually *is* a better Ping-Pong player than you?" Jessica asked.

"Impossible," Steven said flatly.

"But why?" Jessica said. "Just because she's a girl?"

Steven shook his head. "Jess, Jess, Jess. When are you going to understand that there are some things men are naturally superior at?"

"Such as?" Elizabeth challenged him.

Steven set the cake and milk down on the table and straddled a kitchen chair. "Such as sports, or science, or driving, or anything mechanical, or—" He paused to think.

"Or eating," Jessica added with a smirk.

"Or trashing the bathroom," Elizabeth said.

Jessica grinned. "Or burping."

"Or how about bragging?" Elizabeth suggested.

"Absolutely," Jessica agreed.

"You can laugh now all you want," Steven said. "But just wait until the big rematch."

"My money's on Cathy," Jessica said.

"Mine, too," Elizabeth added.

"Fine." Steven crossed his arms over his chest. "You want to bet? I'll wager my next month of trash duty against your next month of table-setting."

"Both of us?" Elizabeth asked.

"You got it."

The twins looked at each other and nodded. "You're on, Steven," Elizabeth said.

"And may the best man win," Jessica added. "Even if he turns out to be a woman!"

"Jessica, could I see you for a minute?" Mr. Baker asked as Jessica came rushing into the SOAR! classroom on Thursday morning.

"But I made it in time," Jessica said. "I was

in the door when the bell rang." She waved her arm. "I have all these witnesses, Mr. Baker."

"This isn't about being late," the teacher replied with a grin. "I'm late sometimes myself. Every now and then you have to stop and smell the flowers." He waved a white slip of paper in the air. "Come, come."

Jessica glanced over at Elizabeth and shrugged. Then she followed Mr. Baker to the doorway.

"A messenger just brought this to me," he said, lowering his voice. "Apparently Mr. Clark wants to see you in his office immediately."

Jessica felt her heart drop to her toes. "Why would the principal want to see me?" she whispered.

Mr. Baker smiled kindly. "I'm sure you two can straighten things out, Jessica. Just tell him the truth. It's always worked for me."

"But what about the field trip to the Museum of Natural History?" she asked.

"The bus won't roll without you," he promised. "Now, scoot."

Jessica took the white slip and made her way slowly toward Mr. Clark's office. What could Mr. Baker have meant about telling the truth? Did he know something he wasn't telling her?

All the way down the hall, she tried to think of reasons Mr. Clark might want to see her. She'd gotten a lot of detentions lately, of course. But usually Mr. Clark handled more important matters. There had to be something else she'd done, something really horrible.

Then she remembered. Last week in the locker room after gym class she and Lila had started a hair spray war. It wasn't the first time they'd had a "hair raid," but it had been one of their better efforts. Pretty soon everyone had joined in. By the time Ms. Langberg, the gym teacher, had arrived to break things up, the locker room was so full of hair goop that people could hardly breathe. It had been great.

Jessica threw back her shoulders and walked briskly the rest of the way down the hall. How much could Mr. Clark punish her for a little wasted hair spray, after all? She pushed open the door to the principal's office.

"Hello, Jessica," Mrs. Knight said without smiling. "Mr. Clark's been waiting for you. Go right in."

Jessica paused in front of Mr. Clark's door and took a deep breath before stepping inside.

"Jessica," Mr. Clark said in his deep, gravelly voice. He was sitting behind his desk with his hands clasped on top of a manila folder—a folder with her name on it in big red letters. "Please sit down."

Jessica perched meekly on the edge of a chair.

"I think you know why I've asked you here today, don't you?"

Jessica nodded. "And I'm really sorry about it too, Mr. Clark."

Mr. Clark rubbed his chin thoughtfully. "Do you really think saying you're sorry is enough, considering the severity of the violation?"

"Um, no," Jessica said softly, hoping it was the right answer. "I guess not."

"You've betrayed yourself, Jessica," Mr. Clark said, shaking his head. "And you've betrayed the school."

Jessica cleared her throat. It seemed to her that Mr. Clark was getting a little too worked up over some hair spray. Still, she wasn't exactly in a position to argue with him. "I could clean it up," she offered.

"The damage has already been done, young lady."

Damage? How much damage could some mousse do in a locker room? What did it do, eat the paint off the floor? If that were the case she'd be bald by now.

"What I'd like to know, Jessica," Mr. Clark said, "is why you felt it was necessary."

Jessica chewed on her lower lip for a moment. "Well," she said slowly, "I guess it all started in the locker room, when Lila said her Super Spray was better than my Mega Mousse. I mean, to begin with, Mega Mousse has a sunscreen in it to protect your hair from the sun's harmful rays—"

"I beg your pardon?" Mr. Clark interrupted.

"It's true," Jessica said eagerly. "Most people don't realize how much the sun can damage your hair."

Mr. Clark rubbed his temples. "I think we've had a communication breakdown here. Maybe we can discuss hair-care products some other time. But right now I want to know why you cheated on the SOAR! aptitude test."

"What?" Jessica exploded. "I didn't cheat on that test, Mr. Clark!" She sighed. "I didn't even *want* to do well on that stupid test."

Mr. Clark pursed his lips. "How do you explain your high score, given the fact that you're just an average student in science?"

"You tell me and we'll both know," Jessica said hotly. She knew she wasn't being polite, but she felt she had to defend herself. "I don't know why I did so well," she continued. "The questions just weren't very hard. They were like little puzzles, you know?" She paused. "What makes you think I cheated, anyway?"

Mr. Clark gazed out of his window. "I have my sources, Jessica."

What did he mean by that? Jessica wondered. "I'll tell you what," she said, sitting up straight. "I'll take that test again if you want, right here in your office where you can watch me. If I do just as well, that'll prove once and for all that I didn't cheat."

For a few moments Mr. Clark sat silently, looking thoughtful. "Well, I'm inclined to believe you, Jessica," he said finally. "Especially since you've offered to take the aptitude test again. But I don't think that will be necessary. Mr. Baker tells me you're doing well in his class, so I'm going to take your word on this."

"That's a relief," Jessica said.

"But just remember," Mr. Clark added. "I'm going to have my eye on you from now on."

"I'll remember," Jessica promised. "May I go now?"

"Of course," Mr. Clark said. "I understand Mr. Baker is taking you on a field trip today."

Jessica nodded and headed for the door.

"Oh, and Jessica?"

"Yes?" she asked, turning around.

"Was there anything else you wanted to tell me about the incident in the locker room?"

Eight

"Hi, everybody," Jessica said. "Can you squeeze in and make room for me?" The Unicorns had all gathered that afternoon at Casey's Place, their favorite ice cream shop.

"I suppose so," Ellen said coolly, easing over on the seat.

"Nice of you to show up, Jessica," Janet said. "We haven't seen much of you lately."

"I was on a field trip today," Jessica explained.

"How very exciting for you," Ellen said, rolling her eyes.

"Ellen, you're not still mad at me for forgetting your birthday, are you?" Jessica asked as she sat down. "I promise I'm going to make it up to you with a really great present, just as soon as I have time to go shopping."

"She's too busy with her new nerd friends right now, though," Lila said scornfully.

Just then Cammi, Randy, and Lloyd walked by the booth. "Hey, Jessica," Lloyd said brightly. "How'd you like that apatosaurus today?"

Jessica glanced around the table at the Unicorns, who were watching her expectantly. "Um, it was OK, I guess," she said under her breath.

"OK?" Randy echoed. "That thing was more than OK! It was incredible!"

"Yeah," Jessica muttered.

"See you tomorrow," Lloyd said. "Hey, by the way, congratulations on the cap."

"What cap?" Lila asked as Lloyd walked away.

"Long story," Jessica replied.

Janet pursed her lips. "This is just what I was afraid of, Jessica! How do you think it looks for us to have the nerd brigade stop by our table?" She shuddered.

"Will you guys lay off?" Jessica said. "I've already had a very tough day. You won't believe what happened."

"What?" Mandy asked, passing her basket of fries to Jessica.

"Mr. Clark called me into his office and accused me of cheating on the SOAR! aptitude test," Jessica said, lowering her voice. "Can you believe it? I was so mad, I actually offered to take the test again, right there in his office, to prove I was innocent."

"I don't blame you for being mad, Jess," Mary said sympathetically.

"So what happened?" Mandy asked. "Did Mr. Clark believe you?"

"I think so," Jessica said, reaching for a handful of Mandy's fries. "But he said he'd be keeping an eye on me."

"How could you be so stupid, Jessica?" Janet cried suddenly.

"What are you talking about?"

"Mr. Clark gave you the perfect opportunity to quit, and you blew it! I can't believe it!"

"After all the trouble we went to," Lila added.

"What do you mean, *trouble*?" Jessica asked.

"I'm surprised you didn't figure it out by now," Lila said, her voice hushed. "Janet and I sent an anonymous letter to Mr. Clark accusing you of cheating."

"You *what*?" Jessica cried. "Why would you do that?"

"We thought we were doing you a favor," Janet replied angrily. "You wanted out of SOAR!, and we promised you we'd come up with a plan."

"But—" Jessica began.

"Hey, Jess," a boy's voice called out. "Where's the Superstar cap?"

Jessica turned around to see Denny approaching the booth. "Hi, Denny," she said.

"Have a seat, Denny," Janet said, batting her eyelashes.

"Can't stay," he said. "I've got a ton of homework. So do you, Jess, come to think of it."

"Don't remind me."

"So where's the SOAR! cap? I've got to admit I was impressed when you won it again today. Not bad for a puny sixth grader."

Jessica grinned. "Thanks, Denny. That really means a lot to me, coming from a moldy old eighth grader like you!"

"Will somebody please explain what all this cap talk is about?" Ellen demanded in an exasperated tone.

Jessica reached into her backpack and pulled out the SOAR! cap.

"SOAR! Superstar," Lila read. She shrugged. "You're not actually going to wear that, are you, Jessica?"

"I already did," Jessica said defensively. "All day at the museum."

"Gross," Lila exclaimed. "I can't believe you wore that thing in public."

"Why shouldn't I have?"

"First of all, because it's incredibly stupid," Lila answered. "And second of all, because green really isn't your color, Jess."

"You don't understand," Denny interrupted. "Mr. Baker lets the person who gives the most intelligent answer of the day wear the cap until the next class. I know it sounds lame, but it's really kind of an honor."

"So what did you say that was so intelligent, Jessica?" Belinda asked.

"This morning before we left for the field trip, Mr. Baker asked us what a person needs more than anything to be a good scientist," Denny replied.

"How about a microscope?" Lila ventured.

Denny shook his head.

"White mice?" Janet joked, batting her eyelashes at Denny.

"Nope." Denny smiled at Jessica. "Imagination."

"But that's a trick question," Ellen protested. "Who'd ever come up with an answer like that?"

"Jessica did," Denny said, casting her a smile. "Well, I gotta hit the road," he said. "See you tomorrow, Jess."

As soon as Denny was gone, Janet leaned

across the table, her dark eyes flashing angrily. "That's it. You've got to quit SOAR!, Jessica," she commanded.

Jessica stared at Janet in disbelief. "Since when do you make decisions for me?"

"Since right now," Janet shot back.

"I'm sick and tired of people telling me where I don't belong," Jessica said. "Steven, and Mr. Clark, and you—this is *my* decision, not yours." She took a deep breath. "And I'm not quitting SOAR!."

A hush fell over the group. "Listen to me, Jessica Wakefield," Janet said at last. "It's impossible to be both a Unicorn and a dweeb. You're going to have to choose between SOAR! and us."

"But Janet—" Mary started to protest.

"No buts," Janet interrupted with a wave of her hand.

"What gives you the right to make me choose?" Jessica cried.

"I'm the president of the Unicorns," Janet said evenly. "Or maybe you'd forgotten that. It's been so long since you've spent any time with us."

"Janet, this isn't fair!" Jessica said angrily.

"Jessica's right, Janet," Belinda spoke up.

"No, she's not. I agree with Janet," Ellen said.

"Who cares who you agree with?" Mandy exclaimed.

"I care," Lila said.

"Well, who cares if you care?" Mandy shot back.

"Quiet!" Janet shouted, pounding on the table for order. "Do you see what you've done to us, Jessica?" she demanded. "You're tearing the Unicorns apart. Have you ever seen us argue this way before?"

"How about when you wanted to put anchovies on the pizza we ordered at Tamara's sleepover?" Ellen suggested.

"Shut up, Ellen," Janet snapped. She turned back to Jessica. "I'm giving you two days to decide, Jess," she said. "We'll have an emergency meeting on Saturday, and you can announce your decision then. It's up to you. Do you want to be a Unicorn—or a social outcast?"

Jessica jumped up and grabbed her backpack. "I can't believe you're doing this to me, Janet," she cried. "I've always been a loyal Unicorn!"

"Well, now you're a loyal dweeb, too," Ellen said.

"This is ridiculous!" Jessica protested.

"It's SOAR! or the Unicorns," Janet said firmly. "You can't have both. You decide."

Nine

"Today was without a doubt the worst day of my entire life," Jessica said as she stomped into Elizabeth's bedroom.

"Jess, what happened?" Elizabeth asked in surprise.

Jessica flopped onto the bed. "Janet just gave me two days to decide between the Unicorns and SOAR!."

"But that's crazy!" Elizabeth cried.

"*I* know it's crazy, and *you* know it's crazy, but try telling that to Janet," Jessica said. "What am I going to do? I mean, I know the choice should be obvious—"

"You mean staying in SOAR!?"

"No!" Jessica said. "I mean choosing the Unicorns. They mean everything to me, Elizabeth. After you, they're my best friends in the world."

"Some friends," Elizabeth muttered.

"I can understand why they're upset with me," Jessica said. "I've hardly seen them at all this whole week. And I *have* been spending a lot of time with—you know. Non-Unicorns."

"Thank you for not saying geeks," Elizabeth said. "And you know, Jess, those non-Unicorns are more like you than you realize."

"But that's what I'm afraid of!" Jessica cried. "What if I *am* just like them, deep down inside? What if I really *am* smart, Lizzie? I'd never live it down."

Elizabeth tried not to smile. "First of all," she said, "you *are* smart. I mean, it's only natural. You're my twin, after all. But it's nothing to be embarrassed about, Jess. Being smart is a gift. You should use your brains, not hide them. Don't you kind of enjoy feeling smart and special?"

Jessica gave a little nod. "Well, kind of, now that you mention it."

"And can you give me one good reason why you should let the Unicorns push you around like this?"

Jessica shook her head and sighed. "It's easy for you to say, Elizabeth. You're not a Unicorn.

You don't understand what I'd be giving up if I dropped out."

Elizabeth nodded. "It *would* be a tragic waste of all that purple clothing in your closet."

Jessica tossed a pillow at her twin. "I'm serious!" she yelled, but she couldn't help smiling.

"Have either of you talked to Amy lately?" Elizabeth asked Maria Slater and Sophia Rizzo the next day in the hallway before lunch.

"I tried to call her last night," Sophia said, pulling on the brim of the SOAR! cap, which she'd won that morning. "But her mother said she couldn't come to the phone."

Elizabeth sighed. "I guess she's been busy practicing her Boosters routine. But every time I try to talk to her at school, she runs off. I feel like she's avoiding me."

"I wonder if she feels left out because of SOAR!?" Maria suggested.

"That's what I'm afraid of," Elizabeth said. "I tried to talk to her about it, but she got really angry with me. I wish there were some way we could make her feel better."

"I've got a great idea!" Sophia exclaimed. "Why don't we have a sleepover tonight? That would be sure to cheer Amy up."

"Sophia, you're brilliant!" Elizabeth said happily. "Why didn't I think of that?"

"Hey," Sophia said with a grin. "I'm the one with the SOAR! cap on, after all!"

"Does everyone have a shovel?" Mr. Baker asked the SOAR! class on Friday afternoon.

Everyone nodded.

"Excellent," Mr. Baker said. He was wearing faded overalls with his usual high-top tennis shoes. "Now we're going to go out behind the gym and plant saplings. One tree for each of us. Why are we doing this, Winston?"

"Um, because there are fewer and fewer trees each year?" Winston answered.

"And why do we care if there are fewer and fewer trees each year, Denny?"

"Because trees are part of our environment," Denny said.

"A little vague, Denny, but I can't disagree," Mr. Baker said with a smile. "And what is it that trees do, Lloyd?"

"Trees turn carbon dioxide into oxygen," Lloyd said confidently.

"Oh, you're all doing so well!" Mr. Baker exclaimed happily.

Jessica had known all the answers. It was amazing, but for once in her life she hadn't been worried about being called on to give an answer in class. In fact, she looked forward to it.

She glanced down at the bright purple laces of her high-tops. As much as she liked SOAR!, was it worth losing the Unicorns over? Without them her life would seem totally empty. No more meetings. No more Boosters. No more Unicorner. No more purple.

Suddenly Jessica felt a tapping on top of her head. It was Mr. Baker. "Is anybody home in there?"

"W-what?" Jessica stammered.

"I asked you why we don't want too much carbon dioxide in the atmosphere," Mr. Baker said.

Jessica was flustered. She knew the answer, but for some reason her worrying about the Unicorns had driven it right out of her head. "I, uh, I guess I don't know," she muttered, looking down at the floor.

Mr. Baker shook his head. "Because carbon dioxide can trap the sun's light and heat up the whole planet. And then Earth might end up as hot and unpleasant as Venus."

Jessica felt herself blush. She *had* known the answer.

"Everyone ready?" Mr. Baker asked the class. "All right then, we're off to plant the SOAR! forest!"

Mr. Baker led the class down the hallway to a back door. When they reached the grassy area behind the gym, they saw two men unloading trees from a red pickup truck. Each tree was about three feet tall, and the roots were wrapped in burlap sacks.

"Everyone pick out a tree," Mr. Baker instructed. "Then start digging. The hole should be about three feet deep and three feet wide."

"This is kind of like picking out a Christmas tree," Elizabeth remarked as she and Jessica scanned the row of saplings.

"Except that these trees will last longer," Jessica pointed out.

Elizabeth nodded. "I guess I like this one," she said, picking up a tall, thin tree with a scattering of leaves.

As Jessica examined the remaining trees, she noticed a small, scrawny sapling with one lone leaf. She put her hand around its trunk. It wasn't much thicker than a baton. "Come on, tree," she said. "Let's go dig you a new home."

Jessica dragged the tree over to a spot by the corner of the gym building. "This is a good place, tree," she said. "If I plant you here, you can look in both directions."

"All right, everyone, before you start to dig,

you should make sure your trees are at least ten feet apart," Mr. Baker said. "Sophia and Nora, you're so close together that your trees will practically be on top of each other when they grow up. Spread out. And don't plant too close to the gym walls. These trees may grow to be twenty feet tall someday, and they'll need lots of room."

Jessica quickly discovered that the ground was very hard. By the time the final bell rang, her hole was only about half the size it needed to be.

"I guess we'll have to finish up on Monday," Mr. Baker said, sounding disappointed. "The trees should be OK out here as long as the temperature doesn't drop too low at night."

"What if it does?" Elizabeth asked.

Mr. Baker shrugged. "The roots could be damaged. Trees should be in the ground, after all."

"I'm staying until I'm finished planting," Elizabeth said.

Jessica stared at her tiny tree. "Me, too," she added quickly. Most of the other students decided to stay as well.

"OK, if that's what you want," Mr. Baker said, grinning. "Dig on, then."

Jessica began digging again. By the time the hole was deep enough, her hands were red and sore. As she began unwrapping the burlap around her little tree's roots, she thought she heard familiar voices nearby. But she was concentrating too hard to pay much attention to them.

"OK, in you go," Jessica said. She dragged the sapling the last few inches to the edge of the hole and eased it in. The tree lodged in the hole, leaning sideways slightly.

"Now we just have to straighten you out and fill in the hole," Jessica said. She began packing a mixture of dirt and fertilizer around the roots of the tree. "One, two, three, four, fill in my tree's hole some more," she chanted under her breath.

Suddenly Jessica froze. She strained her ears and heard the sound of chanting coming through the wall of the gym. "One, two, three, four, Sweet Valley Middle is ready to score!"

Boosters! She'd totally forgotten!

Jessica dropped her spade and sprinted toward the gym door. Suddenly she stopped in her tracks. She held out her hands and looked at them. They were filthy. Then she looked down at her shoes, which were covered with mud, and at the dirty patches on her jeans.

There was no way she could go into the gym looking like this. By the time she got cleaned up and changed into her uniform, practice would probably be over.

"It's true," Jessica moaned. "Janet's right. I *am* a nerd!" She felt as if she were going to cry.

"Are you OK?"

Jessica glanced up to see Mr. Baker. She quickly wiped away a stray tear with the back of her muddy hand. "Um . . . I guess so."

"Anything you feel like talking about?" he asked, looking concerned.

"It's kind of hard to explain," Jessica said miserably. "I don't think you'd understand."

Mr. Baker smiled. "That's just a hypothesis. Why don't you try me?"

Jessica shrugged. If she was going to be a nerd, she'd better get used to talking to teachers— soon they'd probably be the only ones who *would* talk to her. She took a deep breath. "Well, it's like this. . . ."

Ten

◇

"I haven't been to a sleepover in ages!" Sophia exclaimed as she spread out her sleeping bag on the floor of the Wakefields' family room.

"Me neither," Melissa said.

Elizabeth set a huge bowl of popcorn on the coffee table. "I thought maybe later it would be fun to watch some movies." She pointed to the stack of videotapes on the VCR. "I have to warn you, though. Steven helped me pick them out. I take no responsibility for *Slime Mummies from Venus.*"

Maria grabbed a handful of popcorn. "Maybe we should watch that one first," she suggested with a grin. "After all, we learned a lot about Venus this week in Mr. Baker's class. It might be educational."

Melissa unrolled her sleeping bag next to Sophia's. "I'm really going to be sorry when SOAR! ends next week," she said. "Mr. Baker is such a great teacher."

"I know what you mean," Sophia agreed. "I've actually started thinking maybe I'd like to be a zoologist someday. I've always loved animals, but I never thought of myself as the scientist type, you know?"

"I don't think there *is* a scientist type," Elizabeth said as she stretched out on the couch. "That's another thing I've learned from Mr. Baker."

"Hey, where's Jessica?" Maria asked. "I haven't seen her since we got here."

"I know this is hard to believe," Elizabeth said, "but I think she's upstairs, reading ahead in our SOAR! textbook. She told me she couldn't wait to find out what we'd be learning next!"

For the next hour, the girls ate popcorn and talked about SOAR!. It was almost eight o'clock before Elizabeth looked at the clock and realized that Amy hadn't shown up yet.

"I can't believe Amy still isn't here," she exclaimed. "We've been so busy talking, I sort of forgot about her."

"She did say she was coming, didn't she?" Sophia asked.

"Yes, but I have to admit she didn't sound very enthusiastic," Elizabeth replied. She jumped up and ran to the phone. "I'd better call her," she said. She dialed Amy's number, drumming her fingers anxiously on the receiver while she waited for an answer. Finally Mrs. Sutton picked up the phone.

"Hi, Mrs. Sutton," Elizabeth said. "It's me, Elizabeth. I'm calling to see if Amy's on her way over here yet."

Mrs. Sutton cleared her throat. "I'm sorry, Elizabeth," she said gently. "I don't think Amy's planning on joining you this evening."

"May I talk to her?" Elizabeth asked.

"She says she doesn't feel like talking to anyone right now."

"She's OK, isn't she?"

"I'm sure she'll be fine by Monday," Mrs. Sutton replied.

"Well, will you tell her we miss her?" Elizabeth asked.

"Of course, dear."

Elizabeth hung up the phone, shaking her head.

"What's wrong?" Maria asked. "Isn't Amy coming?"

"She won't even talk to me," Elizabeth said glumly, sinking into an easy chair. "I feel terrible.

All week long I've been so preoccupied with SOAR!, I've hardly spoken a word to Amy. I wouldn't blame her if she's really mad at me."

"She missed our *Sixers* meeting this week, too," Sophia pointed out. "That definitely isn't like Amy."

"I have an idea," Elizabeth said. "Why don't one of you call her? Maybe it's just me she doesn't want to talk to."

"I'll try," Melissa volunteered, leaping up. "What's her number?"

Elizabeth crossed her fingers as Melissa dialed. But Amy didn't want to talk to Melissa, either. Sophia and Maria each tried calling, too, but Amy still wouldn't come to the phone.

"Maybe we should just leave her alone this weekend," Sophia suggested as the girls headed into the kitchen.

"Hey, save me some cookies, Elizabeth," Jessica yelled, hurrying into the kitchen. "Hi, guys. Where's Amy?"

"She canceled on us," Sophia said.

"Uh-oh." Jessica shook her head. "She really *is* in a bad mood. I called Lila a while ago to apologize for missing Boosters practice this afternoon, and she said Amy refused to practice her baton routine in front of them. Amy told them that she'll do it Monday at the district game if she feels like it. Janet was furious."

"What are the Boosters going to do if Amy won't perform at the game?" Sophia asked.

"It's too late for them to come up with a new routine," Jessica said. "So I guess they're just going to hope for the best." She took a glass out of the cupboard and poured herself some lemonade. "I'm not sure I care, anyway. I may not even be a Booster by Monday."

Sophia frowned. "What do you mean, Jess?"

"The Unicorns are making Jessica choose between them and SOAR!," Elizabeth explained. "She has to tell them her decision tomorrow morning."

"You're choosing SOAR!, aren't you?" Maria asked.

"Well, I talked things over with Mr. Baker this afternoon," Jessica answered with a mysterious smile. "Let's just say I have a secret plan."

The girls were still in the kitchen when Steven came bounding up the basement stairs a few minutes later. He dashed into the kitchen breathlessly, with Cathy at his heels. "You are looking at the official reigning Ping-Pong champion of Sweet Valley!" he cried. He clasped his hands together over his head and circled the kitchen table like a prizefighter circling the ring.

"He *beat* you, Cathy?" Elizabeth asked.

"Fair and square, I'm afraid," she said apologetically.

"But we were counting on you, Cathy!" Jessica moaned. "This means we have to take out the trash for an entire month!"

"Sorry," Cathy said, sighing.

"It was no contest," Steven said.

"But she destroyed you the last time you played," Jessica pointed out.

"That was just a fluke," Steven said. He draped his arm around Cathy's shoulders and gave her a kiss on the cheek. "I must say you're being very gracious about this, Cath."

"That makes one of us," she said. "If you don't stop rubbing it in, I may have to ask for another rematch."

Steven laughed. "There's no point in your being humiliated twice," he said, heading for the door. "I'm going to go call Joe Howell and give him the news. He's been bugging me all week about losing to a girl."

"Boys!" Cathy exclaimed as she watched Steven hurry out. "Why is winning so important to them?"

"It's probably just as well you lost, Cathy," Jessica said. "Janet Howell says that guys don't like girls who can do things better than they can."

"That's crazy, Jessica," Sophia said.

"Maybe so, but she swears it helps to play dumb."

"Maybe she's not *playing* dumb," Maria said with a wry grin.

Cathy sighed. "You guys are making me feel terrible." She sat down at the table. "Can you all keep a secret?"

"Sure we can!" Jessica replied. "Spill it!"

"The truth is, I *let* Steven win that Ping-Pong game," Cathy admitted.

"But why?" Elizabeth asked.

"I knew how much it meant to him to win," Cathy replied. "But now he's gloating so much, I'm starting to wonder if I made a mistake."

"You *did* make a mistake!" Jessica cried. "If you don't tell him the truth, Cathy, Elizabeth and I are going to be stuck with a month of trash duty!"

Cathy smiled. "I guess I did kind of let you down. And I have to admit"—she paused, checking the door to make sure Steven wasn't listening—"your brother is being a royal pain about winning."

"Totally obnoxious," Elizabeth agreed.

"On the other hand," Cathy continued, "he was so excited—"

"Here I am!" Steven interrupted, striding into the room. "The King of Ping!"

Everyone stared at Cathy, waiting for her to confess. Instead, she just smiled sweetly. "How about a root beer?" she asked.

"So kind of you to show up, Jessica," Janet said in an icy voice when she opened her front door on Saturday morning.

"Sorry I'm late," Jessica apologized. "My mom drove me over to the mall first so I could pick up this present for Ellen." She held up a little box wrapped in purple tissue paper.

"Better late than never," Janet said, turning and starting up the stairs. "Come on. We're all waiting to hear your decision."

When Jessica entered Janet's bedroom, the Unicorn meeting was already in full swing. Kimberly Haver was talking on the lavender telephone. Mary and Ellen were watching music videos on the portable TV on Janet's desk. Tamara was sitting on the floor, concentrating very hard on her toenails, which she was painting purple. In the background, the radio blared.

"Hi, everybody," Jessica said nervously, setting Ellen's gift down on the bed.

Everyone turned to stare, waiting expectantly.

"Hi, Jessica," Mandy finally said, breaking the silence. She waved the curling iron she was holding. "I'm giving Belinda a makeover."

Mary turned down the sound on the TV set. "Glad you're here, Jess," she said. "We were beginning to get worried you weren't going to show up."

"Like you didn't show up yesterday," Lila said.

"I was planting a tree," Jessica explained.

"How noble of you," Janet said. She sat down on the edge of her bed and crossed her arms over her chest. "So have you made your decision?"

Jessica swallowed. She took a deep breath and tried to recall everything Mr. Baker had told her yesterday.

Jessica stepped over Tamara and stood in the middle of the room. "Yes, I *have* made a decision," she said. "But first I want to talk to you about something else."

"Like what?" Janet demanded.

"Like science."

Most of the Unicorns groaned.

"Save the science for your geek friends," Ellen said with a yawn.

"Really, Jess," Tamara agreed. "Just get to the point."

Jessica walked over to Janet's nightstand, where the radio was blaring. "This *is* the point," she said firmly, pulling the plug on the radio.

"Hey," Lila complained. "That was Johnny Buck. I love that song."

"You would never even have heard of that song if it weren't for scientists," Jessica said.

Lila rolled her eyes. "Give me a break."

Jessica walked over to the phone and yanked the receiver out of Kimberly's hand.

"Hey!" Kimberly protested.

"Kimberly will have to call you back," Jessica said into the receiver. She hung up.

"That was Devin Campbell!" Kimberly cried. "And I think he was just about to ask me out, Jessica!"

"I thought you called to ask if you could borrow his notes from English class," Ellen said.

"One thing might have led to another," Kimberly sulked. "But now I'll never know, thanks to Jessica." She scowled. "I hope you choose the nerds, Jessica. You deserve each other."

Jessica gathered up her courage and walked over to the light switch. Without a word, she flicked it off.

"What are you *doing*, Jessica?" Mandy asked. "Conserving electricity or something?"

"I'm trying to prove that even you guys need science," Jessica said, marching over to Mandy and Belinda.

"That's OK," Mandy said, grinning. "I get the idea." She pulled the plug on the curling iron.

"But I'm only half curled!" Belinda complained.

"Without science, you'd be stuck with straight hair," Jessica said. She returned to the middle of the darkened room while the Unicorns watched her in stunned silence. "Look," she said, "scientists can be geeky, I admit it. But without them, life would be awfully boring. We wouldn't have TV, or VCRs, or radio, or stereos. We wouldn't have makeup, either. Remember what we learned about the pioneers? They had to crush berries and rub them on their faces for blush. Not anymore, thanks to scientists. Without them, things like Mega Mousse would just be a distant dream." She paused for a minute to let her words sink in.

The Unicorns were still staring at her silently. Jessica cleared her throat and continued. "And scientists are cleaning up the air we breathe and the water we drink," she said. "Who knows what they'll come up with next? Lloyd's already working on a homework machine. Someday, scientists may even find a cure for zits."

"Wow," Ellen murmured, touching a pimple on her chin. "That *would* be awesome!"

"I'll tell you something else," Mandy said quietly. "Without science, I probably wouldn't be sitting here today." Mandy had had cancer. The treatments had caused all her beautiful long hair to fall out for a while, but she was well again now—thanks to medical science.

"So I guess what you're trying to tell us is that your science class is more important than we are," Lila cut in.

"No, that's not what I'm saying at all," Jessica said quickly. "I know I've missed some Unicorn stuff this week, and I'm really sorry." She reached for the present she'd brought and handed it to Ellen. "I'm especially sorry I forgot your birthday, Ellen," she said. "I hope this will help make it up to you."

Ellen accepted the present with a shrug. While everyone watched, she tore off the tissue paper and opened the box. Inside was a beautiful purple wallet.

"It's that wallet I saw at Leggett's!" Ellen exclaimed happily. She held it up for everyone to see.

"We can't see it very well with the lights off," Kimberly grumbled.

"But this cost a fortune, Jess!" Ellen said.

"It wiped out my savings," Jessica admitted. "But it was worth it."

"Please stay in the Unicorns," Ellen pleaded. "You gave me the best present of anybody."

"Oh, great!" Lila said with a scowl. "So I guess *my* present wasn't good enough for you?"

"I *want* to stay," Jessica said. "That's what I've been trying to tell everybody. Being a Unicorn means more to me than anything."

"So you've decided!" Mary exclaimed. "Thank goodness. I was afraid we'd lost you, Jess."

Jessica held up her hands. "Wait a second," she said. "I *do* want to be a Unicorn. But I want to stay in SOAR!, too. And I really believe that I can be a good Unicorn without giving up on science." She shrugged. "What can I say? I'm a woman of many talents. Don't you want well-rounded Unicorns in the club?"

"Jessica's right," Mandy spoke up. "She can do both. I for one am proud to have such a smart Unicorn around. And who knows? Maybe Jess will be the one to come up with a cure for zits!"

"Or frizzy hair," Belinda added, shaking her half-straight, half-curly hair.

"Welcome back, Jess," Tamara said.

"I wasn't really gone," Jessica pointed out, grinning.

"Well, you were always at the planetarium or

the museum or somewhere," Tamara said. "It *felt* like you were gone."

"We really missed you at the Unicorner during lunch," Ellen added. "There was no one around to give our leftovers to."

"As far as I'm concerned, you can stay in the club," Kimberly said. "*If* you promise to call Devin and explain that you were suffering from a case of temporary insanity."

"I promise," Jessica said happily.

"Enough, already!" Janet cried, jumping off the bed. "You still haven't made a choice, Jessica. I said it was the Unicorns *or* SOAR!. You can't have both."

"But why not?" Mandy demanded.

"Because I said so!" Janet snapped.

"Janet," Ellen exclaimed, "weren't you listening to Jessica? What about radios and TV's and zits?"

Janet walked over to her bedroom door and pointed to the hall. "This meeting is for Unicorns only," she said coldly. "Jessica, I'm going to have to ask you to leave."

Jessica looked around the room at her friends. Everyone seemed to be on her side—except Janet.

"Shouldn't we take a vote or something?" Belinda suggested.

Janet sent Belinda a threatening glare. "Unicorn rules say I can dump any member I choose," Janet said. "*Any* member."

"What Unicorn rules?" Ellen asked. "We don't have any—"

"Shut up, Ellen!" Janet commanded. "We do now! Are you leaving, Jessica, or will I have to—"

"I'm leaving," Jessica said angrily. She strode past Janet. "And it's your loss."

Eleven

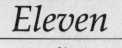

"Hey Jess, how about a little one-on-one with the Ping King?" Steven asked as Jessica stomped through the kitchen later that morning. He lobbed a Ping-Pong ball against the refrigerator.

"Forget it, Steven," Jessica snapped. She caught the ball in her right hand as she walked by.

"I understand," Steven said. "You're afraid of being humiliated by the master."

Jessica walked over to the sink to pour herself a glass of water. She was still stinging from her confrontation with Janet, and she was definitely not in the mood for Steven's bragging. "It's amazing you can fit through the door with an ego that big," she muttered.

"I could give you some extra points so you'd

have a shot at winning," Steven offered. "A *long* shot."

Jessica dangled the Ping-Pong ball over the garbage disposal. "One more word, and it dies a very painful death," she warned.

"Don't do it!" he cried. "That's our last Ping-Pong ball!"

Jessica tossed him the ball. "Go bother someone else, OK?" She glanced at the clock. It was only eleven-thirty, but she felt like crawling back into bed. She'd planned to go shopping with the Unicorns that afternoon. What was she going to do with herself now that she was no longer one of them? Sit home and read books about science all day? What did nerds do with themselves on the weekend? She'd have to ask Elizabeth.

"So you don't want to play even one game?" Steven asked.

"Not in this lifetime."

Steven shrugged. "I guess I could try Cathy, but there's no fun in trouncing her. I've already done it."

"Steven, would you mind just leaving me alone?" Jessica said grumpily.

"I will, as soon as you admit I was right about men being naturally superior to women—"

"Steven, Cathy *let* you win!" Jessica exploded.

Steven's jaw dropped. "No way!"

"*Yes* way," Jessica snapped.

"You're just saying that to get rid of me."

"OK, Steven," Jessica said with a sigh. "You're right. I was just making it up. Cathy lost and you won. Now will you leave me alone?"

Steven turned to go, then stopped. "Are you telling me the truth? Because if you're lying, I'll—I'll . . . I don't know what I'll do, but I guarantee you won't like it."

"I don't think you really *want* to know the truth," Jessica said.

"You're saying she lost on purpose?"

"Yes," Jessica said in an exasperated tone.

Steven slumped into a chair, looking dejected. Suddenly Jessica felt guilty. She hadn't really meant to tell him. But he was being so obnoxious, the words just seemed to fly out of her mouth before she could stop them.

"Look," she said. "Maybe I misunderstood. Cathy was probably just kidding."

Steven shook his head in disbelief. "She *let* me win? Why would she *do* that?"

"I think maybe she thought winning was more important to you than it was to her."

"She *let* me win," Steven repeated. "All this time I've been going around gloating, and you all knew. . . . Boy, now she must think I'm a total jerk."

"Steven, it's just a stupid game," Jessica said soothingly. "Besides, she probably already knew you were a jerk."

"A minute ago I was the Ping King," Steven said sadly. "And now what am I?"

Jessica dropped into a chair next to him.

"You think *you* feel bad," she said. "An hour ago I was a Unicorn. And now I'm just a nerd."

"What's wrong with the three of you?" Mrs. Wakefield asked on Sunday afternoon. "You look like you just lost your best friends."

"That's just about right, Mom," Elizabeth said gloomily.

Steven and the twins were moping in the family room. *Slime Mummies from Venus* was running on the VCR, but nobody was paying much attention to it.

Mrs. Wakefield sat down next to Steven on the couch. "Would somebody mind filling me in?" she asked.

"Well, let's see," Jessica began. "Elizabeth's lost Amy, I've lost the Unicorns, and Steven—" she glanced over at her brother. "I'm not exactly sure what Steven's lost."

"Only my pride," Steven grumbled.

"Cathy was just trying to be nice, Steven," Elizabeth said.

"She shouldn't have lied to me," Steven shot back.

"I'm sure you two will work things out, Steven." Mrs. Wakefield smiled sympathetically. "Elizabeth, have you tried talking to Amy again?"

"I went over to her house this morning," Elizabeth said. "But Mrs. Sutton said Amy still doesn't want to see me." She sighed.

"You may need to give Amy a little more time, Elizabeth," Mrs. Wakefield advised. "Just try to be there for her if she needs you."

"I'm going to go to the game tomorrow afternoon to watch her perform," Elizabeth said. "Maria and I are going to cheer extra loud for her."

"I'm sure she'll snap out of this," Mrs. Wakefield said. "After all, the SOAR! program only lasts another week."

"That's what I kept trying to tell the Unicorns," Jessica said angrily. "Why should I have to give up being a Unicorn for a lifetime over one lousy school week?"

"A lifetime?" Steven repeated. "You actually plan to be a Unicorn when you're an adult?"

"Once a Unicorn, always a Unicorn, Steven," Jessica replied. "Unless, of course, Janet kicks you out."

The phone rang and Mrs. Wakefield picked it

up. "Steven," she said, cupping her hand over the receiver, "it's Cathy."

Steven frowned. "Tell her I'm nursing my fragile male ego."

"Talk to her, Steven," Elizabeth urged.

"Really," Jessica agreed. "There's no point in being a jerk all over again."

Steven sighed. "All right," he said reluctantly. "But I'll take it in the kitchen. I don't feel like having an audience for this one."

"I wish I could tell you what to do about the Unicorns," Mrs. Wakefield said, turning to Jessica. "Maybe if you give them a chance, they'll convince Janet she was being unfair."

"Don't worry, Mom," Jessica said. "I'll get used to being a full-time nerd. Elizabeth's going to give me pointers."

Elizabeth tossed a throw pillow at her twin. Just then, the doorbell rang. "I'll get it," Jessica volunteered. "Before Elizabeth thinks of something heavier to throw."

When Jessica opened the door, she was surprised to see Mandy standing on the front porch. "What are you doing here?" she exclaimed.

"Hi, Jess. Can I come in?"

"Are you sure you should be associating with me?"

Mandy grinned. "I'll risk it. Is there somewhere we can talk? I've got something important to tell you."

Jessica led Mandy up to her bedroom. "If this is about all the nasty things Janet said about me after I left yesterday—" she began.

"It's about Janet," Mandy interrupted. "But it's not what you think." Mandy flopped onto Jessica's bed. "Are you ready?"

"Ready as I'll ever be."

"Well," Mandy said, "after you left the meeting yesterday, everybody was pretty upset at Janet. Most of us thought your speech about science made a lot of sense."

"Mr. Baker gave me the idea for that," Jessica admitted.

"But even more important, we were all relieved to hear that you still care about the Unicorns."

"Of course I care!"

"We were a little worried about all the time you were spending on SOAR!, I guess," Mandy said. She sat up and smiled. "So anyway, we were trying to convince Janet to change her mind, when all of a sudden she started bawling!"

Jessica smiled grimly. "Because she felt so rotten about kicking me out?"

"Not exactly. Because it turns out Janet's jealous of you. She's afraid Denny likes you because you're in SOAR!."

Jessica couldn't help laughing. "But Denny's an eighth grader!" she protested. "He'd never date a sixth grader!"

"Janet isn't in sixth grade," Mandy reminded her.

Jessica flopped down next to Mandy and groaned. "This is crazy! Denny treats me like a little sister!"

"*I* know that, and *you* know that, but I'm not so sure Janet does."

Suddenly Jessica had an idea. "Mandy," she said, "you don't suppose that Janet might change her mind about letting me stay in the Unicorns—"

"—if she knew you weren't interested in Denny?" Mandy finished. "That's funny," she said with a smile. "The same idea just happened to cross my mind."

"Wait, though." Jessica frowned. "What about my being a SOAR! nerd? That's not going to change."

"To tell you the truth, Jess, I don't think that bothered Janet as much as she let on. After all, Denny's in SOAR! too. If anything, I think she was a tiny bit jealous of you for being in SOAR!"

"Jealous?" Jessica echoed in disbelief.

"Sure," Mandy replied. "It sounded like you guys were having so much fun."

"You know what, Mandy?" Jessica said thoughtfully. "I *have* been having a lot of fun, even if a lot of the SOAR! people are—you know, non-Unicorns. The other day at the Natural History Museum, I actually found myself hanging out with Randy and Lloyd."

Mandy smiled. "And having a good time?"

"A great time," Jessica admitted. "When you forget about the highwater pants, those guys can really crack you up. Did you ever hear the joke about the electron and the quark?"

"Say what?" Mandy asked, grinning.

"It's a joke Lloyd told me." Jessica stood up. "Come on, I'll tell you on our way downstairs. I'm pretty sure I smell peanut butter cookies baking. I think my mom was feeling sorry for all of us."

In the hallway, they ran into Steven, who was whistling happily. "Hey, how come you're so happy all of a sudden?" Jessica asked.

"I talked Cathy into another Ping-Pong match. Only this time she promised to play her very best," Steven said. "No more worrying about my fragile ego."

"You sure you can handle it?" Jessica asked.

"Sure I'm sure."

Jessica stared at him doubtfully.

"Well, I'd *prefer* to win," Steven admitted. "But if I lose, I lose. I can take it like a man."

"Good," Jessica said with a grin. "I'm glad to hear it. Because my money's on Cathy all the way!"

Twelve

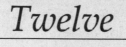

Monday morning before SOAR! class started, Jessica took Denny aside. "Denny?" she said. "Suppose I knew someone who had a serious crush on you. Would you want to know about it?"

Denny gave her a pat on the back. "Look, Jess," he said kindly, "I really like you, too. But just as a friend, you know?"

"Wait a second!" Jessica exclaimed with a laugh. "You don't get it, Denny. Nothing personal, but I like Aaron Dallas."

"But—"

"And you eighth graders think you're so swift!" Jessica teased. "I was talking about Janet Howell."

"Janet?" Denny said. "Really?"

"Really. Trust me on this. I have very reliable sources."

Denny grinned. "That's kind of a coincidence. I was actually thinking about asking Janet out," he admitted.

"Well, would you do me a big favor and get it over with?" Jessica asked. "It would really make my life a whole lot easier."

"I don't get it." Denny shook his head. "What do you get out of the deal?"

"The Unicorns," Jessica said, crossing her fingers. "I hope."

When Jessica emerged from Mr. Baker's class-room at lunchtime, she was surprised to find Janet waiting for her in the hallway.

"Jessica, we need to talk," Janet said in a low voice.

"What about?" Jessica asked. There was no way Denny could have asked Janet out yet. The SOAR! class had been in the lab all morning, look-ing at dust mites under the microscope.

"Just come on, OK?" Janet said irritably. "Someplace private."

They headed for the girls' room, walking side by side in silence. Whatever Janet wanted to say, it couldn't be good, Jessica decided.

Inside the girls' room, Janet led Jessica to a

corner by the sink. "This isn't easy for me to say, Jessica."

"What isn't easy?"

Janet looked down at the floor and muttered something that sounded like "Tuesday."

"What *about* Tuesday?" Jessica asked.

Janet tapped her foot on the floor impatiently. "I said, I'm asking you *to stay*," she growled.

Jessica narrowed her eyes. "To stay in the Unicorns, you mean?"

"No, Jessica," Janet said sarcastically. "To stay cool. Of *course* to stay in the Unicorns!"

"This isn't just because you need me for the Boosters routine this afternoon, is it?"

"The routine's probably already going to be a disaster, anyway. I'm not even sure Amy's going to show up for the game." Janet threw up her hands. "Look, Jess. You want me to get down on my knees and beg?"

"That would be nice."

"Don't hold your breath." Janet smiled. It wasn't much of a smile, but it was a start.

"I don't get it," Jessica said. "Why did you change your mind?"

"I just realized . . ." Janet turned around and stared into the mirror, fixing her hair. "I just realized that the Unicorns are more important than anything." She paused. "Or anybody."

"What made you decide that?"

"Oh, all right," Janet said, throwing up her hands. "I might as well tell you. Yesterday my dad and Joe were trying to figure out how to set up our new VCR. But of course they were getting it all wrong and arguing over everything."

"Janet, what does your new VCR have to do with me?"

"I'm getting to that, do you mind?" Janet snapped. "Anyway, I offered to help them out. And they both tried to tell me that it was a man's job, and way too technical for a girl. Joe said they could figure it out because they were used to using complicated equipment. He said the most complicated thing I ever used was a mascara wand. Only he called it a 'twisty eyelash thing.' "

"I know there must be a point here somewhere," Jessica said, trying not to smile.

"The *point* is, I started telling them about all the scientific stuff I use every day. Like telephones, and hot curlers, and hair dryers, and— well, you get the idea. Then all of a sudden I realized I was repeating everything you said the other day. And worst of all, I realized I'd been telling you the same thing Joe and my dad were telling me—you know, that science is just for guys."

"So you're saying you were wrong?" Jessica asked.

"Don't push it, Jessica," Janet warned.

"So what happened with the VCR?" Jessica asked.

"Well, I read the manual, and I forced them to let me help."

"And you *fixed* it?" Jessica asked excitedly.

"Well, no," Janet admitted. "Actually, all three of us gave up. We got the seven-year-old kid from across the street to do it. He's really into video games, and he set up the VCR in about two minutes."

Jessica shook her head in confusion. "So I'm back in the Unicorns because you got a new VCR?"

"No, Jessica," Janet replied. "You're back in the Unicorns because I'm a *very* reasonable person."

"Do you think she's going to do it?" Elizabeth asked Maria that afternoon. The two girls were sitting near the bottom of the bleachers in the crowded middle school gym. It was half-time, and Sweet Valley Middle School's basketball team was ahead by eight points.

"Your guess is as good as mine," Maria said.

Suddenly the middle school band struck up a

brisk tune. The Boosters marched out onto the gym floor and began a complicated baton routine, while the audience in the bleachers clapped along. Jessica dropped her baton once, but she quickly picked it up and fell back into step.

"Poor Jess," Elizabeth said to Maria. "She's been so busy with SOAR! this past week that she hasn't had much time to practice."

"I don't see Amy," Julie Porter said, looking disappointed. "I guess she chickened out."

But just then Amy burst through the gym doors, cartwheeling across the floor. She took her place in the center of the Boosters and began an intricate series of twirls and tosses.

"She's incredible!" Elizabeth said. The crowd applauded wildly.

As the song came to a close, Amy stepped forward. She seemed to hesitate for a minute, and Elizabeth held her breath. Then Amy threw her baton into the air, so high it nearly touched the ceiling. As it fell back toward her, she managed to do a triple spin before catching it effortlessly.

"Amazing!" Julie yelled. The crowd went crazy.

Amy took a bow, then motioned for the other Boosters to join her. They all bowed together, then ran off the court.

"Let's go congratulate her," Elizabeth said excitedly.

When she, Maria, and Julie reached the locker room, they found Amy surrounded by the other Boosters.

"Amy!" Elizabeth cried, running over to give her a hug. "You were terrific!"

"Do you really think so?" Amy asked breathlessly.

Jessica laughed. "We keep telling Amy she blew everyone away with her routine, but she refuses to believe us."

"Are you kidding, Amy?" Julie cried. "Didn't you hear the crowd?"

"Well, yes." Amy stared at the floor. "But—"

"Trust me, Amy," Mandy broke in, "you were fantastic."

"Why didn't you tell us you'd worked up such an amazing routine?" Belinda asked.

"Well, it didn't start out that way," Amy admitted. "For the first few days, I dropped my baton every single time on that last toss. I was going to just give the whole thing up. But I finally got the hang of it." She looked at Elizabeth and smiled. "I realized that just because you can't do something perfectly all the time doesn't mean you should give up hope. Right?"

Elizabeth put her arm around Amy's shoulders. "Right."

"Janet," Kimberly said, as the Boosters were changing in the locker room after the game, "what's that brown stuff on your face?"

"Brown stuff? The only thing I have on my face is some Magic Mud I borrowed from Jessica." Janet reached up and touched her cheek. "You know, my cheeks do feel kind of funny. Sort of stiff and hard to move." She scowled at Jessica and ran to a mirror. "My face is covered with cement!" she cried. "Jessica, what have you done to me?"

Just then Lila poked her head in the door. "Janet?" she called. "Denny's out here in the hall. He says he has something important to ask you."

"Denny? You're kidding! I can't let Denny see me like this!" Janet screeched. "Jessica, do something! You're the scientist. How do you get this goop off?"

Jessica shrugged. "Search me, Janet. We didn't get into chemistry. That's in high school. I do have one hypothesis—"

"Where is it?" Janet cried. "In your purse? Your locker? Give it to me, Jessica!"

"My hypothesis is that you should try using a whole lot of soap and water," Jessica answered with a laugh.

Janet ran to the sink and began frantically scrubbing at her face. "It's coming off!" she reported.

"There you have it," Jessica said. "Another triumph of modern science!"

"In this corner, we have Cathy 'Killer' Connors," Jessica said, trying to sound like a sports announcer. It was Monday evening, and the great Steven-Cathy rematch was about to begin. "Killer's won one round, and lost one round. Kind of. And tonight she's facing her most challenging match ever."

Cathy bowed modestly at one end of the Ping-Pong table and gave a little wave with her paddle. The audience—Elizabeth, Amy, Lila, and Joe Howell—applauded and cheered.

"And in this corner," Jessica announced, "Steven 'Macho Man' Wakefield!"

Steven came running over, waving his paddle in the air and stopping every few steps to flex his muscles.

"Hey," he complained. "You guys applauded louder for Cathy."

"Here come the refreshments," Mr. Wakefield called out as he and Mrs. Wakefield came down the stairs. Mrs. Wakefield was carrying a huge bowl of popcorn.

"Please, no more noise from the audience,"

Jessica said sternly. "These are highly trained ath-
letes and they need total concentration. Mr.
Judge," she said, turning to Joe. "Could you read
us the rules, please?"

Joe grabbed a handful of popcorn out of the
bowl and stood up. "Ladies and gentlemen, this
is a fight to the finish," he said. "Winner takes all.
And the first person to score twenty-one points is
the winner."

"And if I win, you take out the garbage for an
entire month," Steven added, pointing at Jessica.
"Don't forget our little bet."

"How long will this dumb game last?" Lila
demanded. "There's a TV show on in half an hour
that I want to see."

"Can we start already?" Steven asked.

"First we have to flip a coin to see who
serves," Jessica said.

"Oh, Steven can serve," Cathy said.

"Don't do me any favors," Steven warned.
"I'll beat you fair and square."

"Amy?" Jessica called out. "The coin!"

"Oh. The coin." Amy stood up again and
began digging through her jeans pocket. "Now,
what did I do . . ."

"Here," Lila said, sounding exasperated. She
held up a quarter.

Amy flipped the coin in the air.

"Heads!" Steven called.

Amy trapped the falling coin against the back of one hand. "Heads it is."

"Hah!" Steven cried triumphantly. He picked up the ball and gave Cathy a hard stare. "Prepare to be beaten."

Steven served, and Cathy returned the ball. He fired it back and it sailed past Cathy's outstretched paddle.

"Yes! My point!" Steven yelled.

But the next point went to Cathy, and from then on it was an even battle. When the game reached an eleven-to-eleven tie, they took a break for water.

"I don't mean to put pressure on you, Cathy," Jessica whispered. "But I really do hate taking out the garbage."

"Steven's playing very well tonight," Cathy admitted.

"You're not *letting* him win again, are you?" Jessica demanded.

Cathy grinned. "No way!"

When the game resumed, Steven scored three quick points in a row. But then Cathy came back strong, and soon the game had reached a twenty-to-twenty tie.

"The next person to score a point wins," Elizabeth declared.

Jessica raised her hand for silence. "It's down to a single point, ladies and gentlemen. And the crowd is on the edge of their seats!"

"Not Lila," Joe pointed out. "She went upstairs to watch TV."

"You know," Mrs. Wakefield said, "you've both played so well, maybe you should forget about the last point and call it a tie."

"Not a chance." Steven shook his head firmly. "Win or lose, we're playing to the end." He served the ball and it flew so fast that it was almost past Cathy before she could move and block the shot. The ball bounced back hard, heading straight for Steven's face. He brought his paddle up quickly—but not quickly enough.

The ball hit him in the forehead and bounced to the floor.

"Cathy's the winner!" Jessica cried. "No garbage duty, Lizzie!"

"Congratulations, Cathy," Mr. Wakefield said.

Steven walked around the table and shook Cathy's hand. "Good game," he said.

"Wow!" Elizabeth said. "Can that possibly be our very own Steven, being so sportsmanlike about losing to a girl?"

"Oh, I've learned a lot," Steven said humbly.

"That girls can be good at sports, for example?" Jessica said.

"Yes," Steven agreed.

"And that girls can be just as good as boys are at science?" Jessica demanded.

"Absolutely," Steven said meekly. "I now *know* that girls can be really great at science. Maybe even *better* than boys."

"About time," Jessica said with satisfaction.

"In fact," Steven continued, "I think you two are so smart that you could even figure out my freshman biology."

"Of course we could. Couldn't we, Elizabeth?" Jessica said confidently.

"No problem," Elizabeth said.

"Yep." Steven took Cathy's hand and headed for the stairs. "That's why you'll find my biology textbook on the kitchen table. My homework assignment's in the front. I'm going to take Cathy to Casey's for a sundae. Could you two please try to have my homework done by the time I get back?"

Steven grinned and dashed up the stairs.

"You know something, Jess?" Elizabeth said. "I know we're just as smart as Steven. But I get the feeling we were just outsmarted."

"Lizzie," Jessica agreed, "I believe your hypothesis is correct."

"You know, I miss SOAR!," Elizabeth said the following Monday as she walked into art class, "but it's nice to be back to our regular schedule again."

"It's nice to have you back again," Amy replied with a smile. "Although I kind of enjoyed having all that peace and quiet."

Sophia laughed. "I'm beginning to think we missed Amy more than she missed us!"

As the room began to fill, the three girls took their seats. "I wonder what our next art project is going to be?" Sophia asked.

Sarah Thomas twisted around in her seat. "We're finishing those pastels we worked on last week."

"I guess we missed that because of SOAR!," Sophia said.

"But next week we're starting a new project that has something to do with the library," Sarah added.

"The library?" Sophia repeated doubtfully.

Sarah nodded. "That's what Mr. Sweeney told me."

"Well unless we're going to be painting the walls, I think you must have heard him wrong," Sophia said.

"I *didn't* hear him wrong," Sarah replied, sounding a little annoyed.

"Actually, the library could *use* some fresh

paint," Elizabeth interjected. "It *is* a little depressing."

"What do you expect?" Sarah said. "I mean, it's a library. Libraries are always depressing."

"I *love* libraries," Sophia replied. "They're so quiet, and there's that wonderful book smell—"

"Personally, I think libraries should pipe in music," Sarah said. "You know—like a nice rock station."

"That'll be the day!" Amy laughed. "Somehow I can't see Ms. Luster cranking up the Johnny Buck."

Just then Mr. Sweeney walked in. "Hello, folks," he said. "I've got news for you. I've volunteered you for a very special project. The library needs some sprucing up, and Ms. Luster would like you to make some murals."

"See? I told you," Sarah whispered to Sophia with a triumphant smile.

"Start thinking of ideas for a theme," Mr. Sweeney continued. "Next week we'll decide on one. Then I'll divide you into groups of three, and each group will paint one mural."

"How about some kind of science theme?" Sophia suggested. "Maybe from something we learned in SOAR!."

"How boring!" Sarah exclaimed. "I was

thinking of something prettier, like a bunch of rainbows.''

"Rainbows?" Sophia said, wincing. "Are you kidding?"

"I'm sure we'll come up with something great," Elizabeth said confidently. "This project sounds like it's going to be a lot of fun!"

With feuding classmates like Sophia and Sarah, how much fun will the art project really be? Find out in Sweet Valley Twins and Friends #62, SARAH'S DAD AND SOPHIA'S MOM.